BLUEBERRIES

Copyright © 2023 James C. Satterthwaite

All rights reserved.

This book or any portion thereof may not be copied, used, transmitted, or distributed for any purpose without prior written permission by the author, with the exception of short quotations cited in reviews and articles and other noncommercial uses permitted by copyright law. For permission requests, write to the author addressed "Attention: Permission Request" at the email address below.

This is a work of fiction. Any references to historical events, real people, or real places are used fictitiously. Names, characters, and places are products of the author's imagination.

Cover design and graphics © Breyanna I.L. Evans
Book design © James C. Satterthwaite

AzureStar, INK
First printing edition 2024.

jcsatterthwaite.author@gmail.com
@james_c_satterthwaite

To all those people who are afraid of the dark.

James C. Satterthwaite

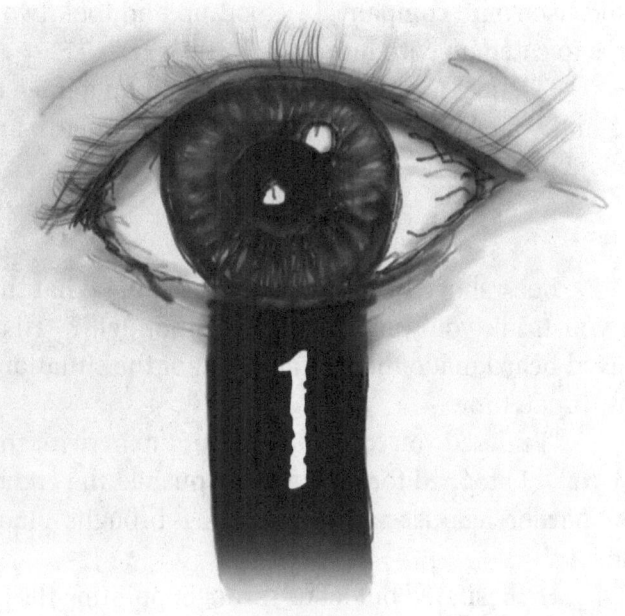

1

Beck's anger was apparent as he waved the double barrel shotgun in my direction. Stevvie stuck his head out from behind my leg to get a gauge on the situation.

... Five Days Ago ...

Stevvie was a six-year-old with a gun in his hand and blood on his shirt, more grown up than most of the adults I'd met before the Finish. His eyes were kind but full of anger and confusion. They had a look about them, one that said - he would shoot me at the slightest sign that he might need to.

I could tell he hadn't eaten in a while, so I reached in my bag and gave him half of a peanut butter and jelly sandwich. His eyes lit up as he scarfed it down. He smiled up at me. Tucking the revolver behind the belt too big to fit him, he waved his hands, began to walk away but he turned back and said, "You coming or what? You look like you could use some company." I stood up and took two large steps to catch up with his stubby little legs.

"Thanks for the food." He picked up a huge duffle bag and water jug, struggling under their weight, and we walked on.

... Present ...

Beck shoved the barrel at my head, "What the hell do you think you're doing on my land, Jelli?" His half-shaved beard made the gun and soul of the situation a bit less threatening.

"I missed you too," I said. "But I'm here for the kid, not you." I stepped forward and he pushed the end of the gun harder against my forehead. "I brought blueberry jam..."

He hesitated but let us through, pointing the gun to direct us toward his front door.

Fresh food was hard to come by in the Finish, and blueberries just happened to be his favorite. Coincidence, maybe, or maybe I knew he'd take in the kid for weekly payments of homemade blueberry jam.

He slathered the dark blue slug of jam on two pieces of toast. Seeing the kid watch him, Beck offered him one of the slices. The kid's face lit up and he took a large bite.

"Blueberries are my favorite." Stevvie said.

Crum-filled jam ran down Stevvie's chin. Beck gave a half smile, then wiped his own face on his sleeve and walked into the bathroom to finish shaving.

His favorite black blade was newly sharpened and he rubbed it across his face. It sliced the hairs on his chin with expected ease. I sat quietly watching. Beck cut himself, a small but deep incision and he continued as if it had not happened.

When he was done, he examined the cut and flushed it with hydrogen peroxide. Then splashed his face with room temperature tap water. He picked a blue stained rag to dry his face from off the bathroom shelf. After staring at his reflection in the mirror, he finally looked at me, ready to talk. He set his left hand on the rim of the little, circular sink, rubbed his face with his right, and pointed at me before talking.

"I can't," he lowered his volume before continuing. "I can't take on another one... I've already got enough of them in my hair as it is. Besides, do you really think he'd make it?" He shifted his weight, noticing my irritation and trying to squirm away from it. "He's small. He's *really* young."

Stevvie was leaning in his chair to see and hear us better, so Beck walked around me and shut the door. He went over to the closed toilet and sat on the lid, setting his elbows on his knees and his face in his hands.

"I don't know if he's strong enough to get there..." He looked out the clouded window "I'm not letting another one die on me. Not again, not like she did..." His voice cut off and he swallowed loudly, trying to fight the heavy tears threatening to fall from his eyes.

I looked at the swinging, flickering ceiling light, it burnt my vision and gave me an excuse for tearing up.

"Blood, water and a revolver." My words pulled both of us out of our trance like thoughts.

"What?" He looked up.

"That's all I found on him." I looked away from the ceiling to make eye contact. "When I first met him, he steadily held a gun between his hands, a gallon of water on the ground at his feet, he had both eyes open and blood spatter on his shirt. He was ready to shoot me... it wasn't a big deal, but I could tell he'd done it before. I could tell he would do what he needed to do to survive." I pushed off the wall and walked closer to him. "He's more likely to make it than you are, old man."

He let himself half smile but it quickly faded with a sigh.

"Fine, but you're coming with me. I don't change pull-ups for strange little punks." He pulled his hands through his dark hair, got off the john, picked up his wash rag and walked into his kitchen. I smiled widely at this, I think it only irritated him more.

Beck stalked to Stevvie's side with judging eyes. Harder than necessary, he set the lightly damp rag on the table.

"Wipe that shit off your face." Beck took a step back as the boy scrubbed the jam from his chin. Then he squatted down to Stevvie's eye level and stuck out his hand. "Gi'me the gun, kid."

"How 'bout you give me yours first?" Stevvie said, sticking his hand out and in front of Beck's face. Beck didn't look as though he enjoyed that, as he stood up ready to fight. His head shook with laughter and his chest heaved.

He slapped his knee and said, "You're a tough kid. But watch yourself. Stubbornness like that could get you killed real quick."

He turned around shaking his head, and he leaned in as he passed me.

"I don't think I hate him. We leave just after sunrise." Off he walked to the back of the house, most likely to turn on the lights. It will be getting dark soon, we all know what happens in the dark.

... Five Years Ago ...

It was warm and sunny. Even though we didn't know it yet, the Finish had started. The news outlets were confused and didn't know how to tell the public, they didn't know what to say, or if they even could without starting up some kind of worldwide panic.

It was a beautiful sunset and the green corn fields lit up like liquid gold under the intense yellow lighting. The sky was a puddle of mixed colors and clouds. A hot breeze shuffled the corn, carrying cotton in its clutches.

I climbed the hill with a glass tupperware bowl of blueberries in hand, bringing them to the house like I did every Tuesday. I reached the top of the hill just in time to see the orange streak drive to the west.

Smash. The sound of glass shattering rang out from inside the house. The bowl from my hands hit the grass padded dirt.

I was running as fast as I could, my legs struggling to push me farther up the hill. My body slammed against the front door. *Stupid deadbolts.* I jumped off the porch, picked up a sturdy rock, and ran in the direction of the kitchen. Stumbling and falling into the frame of the window, I caught myself and looked in.

They were lying on the tile floor. It was dark, and glass lay scattered all around them from the dishes they had held. It looked like they had something on their faces, on their eyes... They were still, as if they were dead...

I hit the window with the rock. Once. Twice. Again and again, I drove the stone to the glass, barely making a chip. But I still had to try.

My hands were raw and my face flooded with tears. Each and every step hurt to take. *My phone, the police.* I lit up with hope and searched my pockets. *It's in the glove box of my car about a mile down the gravel road.*

I picked up running again, adrenaline pushing me forward. Against the wind, against the corn. I was so scared and so confused I only wanted to pull them close to me and keep them safe, all this unknowing, all this distance, like a spike through my chest. *What if* - The truck, the road, I could see it! That sight cut through my brain and tore away my words.

I fell and slid down the entirety of the hill and into the side door. Grabbed the handle and tried to open it. *Locked...* The thought itself felt like an exhale. I fumbled through my pockets and dropped the keys. The lights flashed and the pin popped up. Luck, I guess.

I snatched up the keys and opened the door. I jumped in and leaned over the seat, leaned forward and opened the glove box. Before I knew it, the numbers were dialed. *Voicemail for the police station? I didn't know 911 had a voice mail.*

I pulled back out of the car and stood there staring disbelievingly at my phone. I swore that I heard a noise in the silence of the night, like a scream or something breaking, something that made me look up from my phone...

The city in the distance had been engulfed in glowing flames. The horizon lit up in that violent orange. I stumbled back in fear and shock. *What was going on? Why is it happening? Why are they dead? So many dead...*

... Present ...

I handed Stevvie a fleece blanket and tucked him in. He slept fine in the light, he must have gotten used to it by now. *How long was he out there, how long has he been alone?* Beck was standing in the doorway waiting for me.

"It's been a while..." He said walking with me to the living room.

"What's been a while?"

"Since you've come, especially with a kid his age. How old is he, anyway?" Beck said as we watched the sun set at the broken bay window, just like we used to.

"Six, I think. He doesn't talk much yet, but who does. Who would *want* to talk about their version of the Finish." *Even the two of us don't want to.*

"What about the blood? Do you know whose it is?" The sun finally set, the darkness chasing the orange - and the memory - out of my view.

"No clue. I just hope he found that shirt like that. A kid his age doesn't need the guilt of that. He doesn't need that holding him back." I was lost in my words and Beck was looking at me worriedly. He stood up and turned away.

"Good night. Be ready by dawn." Then he headed for his room, awaiting another sleepless night.

"Good night." I said and got up from the window. I glanced over my shoulder one last time into the still darkness. It was so beautiful, but it hurt to look. It hurt to remember it all.

I laid on a hard dark blue cot on the opposite side of the guest room as Stevvie. Looking up to the blindingly bright lights, I rolled over to face the wall and passed out.

I sat up in a cold sweat. Thinking I was still there, watching Beck put a handful of buck shot in her head, because he knew he'd already lost her. Knew that *we* had already lost her. I walked to the bathroom and splashed cold water on my face to get rid of the memory, the ghost of her blood on me. I couldn't look at myself in the mirror. I haven't been able to, not since that day two years ago.

I walked to the kitchen to grab one of the few beers we had left and found Beck sitting at the table, just looking at a jar of blueberry jam.

"Hey-" He cut me off by throwing the jar at the far wall as hard as he could. It shattered and I jerked back.

"What are you doing?" I whisper yelled at him. "The kid is sleeping!" I walked over to slap him or at least shake some sense into him, but he caught me by the wrist. I expected him to scream and fight, he simply squeezed my hand and sobbed.

I pulled him up off the chair into a hug and helped walk him into his room. I handed him a bottle of well expired sleep medication and a dusty glass of water. He pretended to take some, and I pretended not to notice that he didn't. He set the cups on his night table. I kissed his forehead and went back into the kitchen to clean up the sticky mess.

Neither of us could sleep much; the nightmares wouldn't let us.

It was morning, before the sun. Beck had the bags packed and breakfast made. Little Stevvie was standing and leaning over me, his huge smile beaming a sweet 'good morning'.

"Are you coming to eat breakfast?" His pitch rose with the question, and he skipped out of the guest room before I could respond. I stood up, stretched and walked after him. As I was leaving, I looked at the door jam. *Heights*. There weren't many notches in the wood, but enough that Beck had painted over it in at least one coat of white wall paint.

I ran my finger down the notches, a sad smile sprouting its roots. I shook my head and turned into the kitchen.

"How'd you sleep?" Beck asked, handing me a plate of scrambled pre-chickens.

"Great! How about you guys?" I said sarcastically and changed the focus with a question.

"Me too!" Stevvie said, letting eggs fall out of his mouth with the words and missing the tone of my voice. Beck just nodded and gave a soft, small smile.

"Forget about last night," he whispered to me, "it's not a big deal." I shrugged. I knew he didn't want to talk about it, because I didn't want to either. So I let it be.

The eggs were hot and cheesy and near to melting in my mouth. We all ate slowly, savoring the delicious powdered eggs and hushing our hungered minds one bite at a time.

We were ready to go, bags packed and teeth brushed. The three of us just sat under the porch light and watched the sun rise. It was about a day's walk to the next checkpoint, but Stevvie was already jumping with excitement at the thought of seeing The Camp.

Day One

    I was looking at the ground to avoid the sun burning my eyes. Beck stopped walking and grabbed the kid by the back of his collar. I ran into him and stumbled in reverse. I looked up at his head of hair. I waited for him to turn around and say something, explain himself, but he didn't.

    I moved around the side of him, and he grabbed my arm without looking. His eyes were forward, narrowed. He never shows his emotions, not in the day at least, only in the darkness did he see his demons and let them show. It had been a long time since he showed himself in the light of the sun.

My eyes followed his gaze. How could I have missed it... rattling away like that? It was a snake. Tan with brown, beautifully detailed diamonds lining its body, leading to its rattle. It was coiled up with its fangs exposed and maraca skyward.

Fear flushed my face with blood, and I began to sweat, worrying about that snake so close to Stevvie... *No!* I can't let myself think of that. *Just no.* Then Beck spoke. His strong words brought me back and I looked at him.

"I am going to throw you. Don't worry, the sand is soft, I just want you out of my line of fire." His voice was calm and quiet but deep. He squeezed Stevvie's arm so hard the little boy winced. "One..." Long inhale. "Two..." Exhale and-

Bang. Solid and ear shattering. Beck's hands were still on the boy and his gun still filled its holster. Stevvie's face was calm and collected. The old revolver fit so surprisingly smoothly in his little hands.

The snake's long body lay twitching, writhing around in pooling blood. Pieces of its head decorated the sand. Beck let go of the boy's shoulder.

Beck stood in shock, confused about what had just happened. He looked down at Stevvie almost scared. The speed and accuracy of the shot had made Beck step back a couple of times, as if stumbling. He hadn't ever seen a shot like that, not from a kid, or anyone other than himself for a long time. Seemed like the kid was the only one who could out-shoot Beck Shot.

We were sitting on a large, rough boulder, sinking into a thin strip of shade from a wiry old tree.

"You don't want to have a heat stroke." Stevvie said, as he shuffled through his oversized duffle bag and pulled out a couple half full gallon jugs of water. "Go on, drink up." His face tilted with a sweet smile as he handed us the bottles. I was *really* hoping he would make it to The Camp. Hoping that he might make it out of the Finish, if it had an end.

The water was warm, refreshing and in a way it woke me up more, which was pleasant. We had more water of our own, but we still had miles to go. We had been walking for several hours, and it felt amazing to be able to sit down and make some noise.

Beck liked the quiet, especially when he walked. He said it kept him focused, just in case of an emergency. Honestly, I never believed half the crap he said these days. *I* thought it was because he didn't want to talk. It was hard for him; he had lost more than his share.

Stevvie laid in the hot sun and passed out almost immediately. He was only six, but hadn't complained about the walking. I wanted to give him some time to rest. Not too much though, we were on the clock.

After a short time, Beck stood up with a sigh, walked over to the kid, and tossed me his duffle bag. He leaned over and gently slung the sleeping Stevvie over his shoulder, holding him up with his right arm. It was nice to see this softer side of him.

We kept walking, on and on and on. When we crested that oh so familiar hill of sand, we could see the house, not taller than my thumb, that was the second stop. Just as soon as we did, little Stevvie stretched out his arms and awoke from his slumber. He saw the house, jumped out of Beck's arms and started running down the hill, just happy to see something in the vast plains. I chased after him.

We tripped, falling down the sand. Beck was standing at the top of the hill looking down at us like we were fools to get this excited over an old, broken-down house. He finally got to the bottom of the hill, where we were running in place waiting for him.

"Ready?" I said looking between them. "Set..." They returned the look to me. "Go!" All three of us ran this time. The sand was heavy and beginning to fill our shoes. "Last one there's a rotten egg!"

Beck was a slightly faster runner than me. I was also not running at full power, so that I wouldn't lose Stevvie. Beck rushed past me, scooping up the kid onto his shoulders as he did, smiling back at me. My heart skipped a beat, it had been so long since I had seen a real smile on those lips.

When we got to the front of the shack, we were panting for breath. There is a large difference between "fun running" and "fear running". We hadn't run for fun in who knows how long, and we were laughing and crying, with huge smiles across our faces, even though we were coughing for air. We sat like that for a few moments but were interrupted by heavy, dragging footsteps.

"Quiet now." Beck whispered with a finger over his mouth to hush us. He jumped up and looked, rushed to the door where he put his finger over the peephole. He waited, listening to the bolts and locks unlatch one at a time, one after the other. The door opened and Beck gathered up an old lady into a bear hug, her feet and gun dangling above the ground. His smile widened.

"Put me the *fuck* down!" she yelled, pulling her arm up out of his grip and flipping him off when he put her down, her face was sour as she straightened out her flowery dress. The second she looked up, she saw me, her face softening into a perfect kindness. "Sweet pea, you get more gorgeous every time I see you." She pulled me down into a hug.

When she pulled away, she simply stared at me. Stevvie popped his face out from behind me and gave her a broad smile, and she lit up like the sun at the sight of that adorable face. Her smile radiated kindness as she kneeled to his level. "Now, what's your name, Sunshine?"

"Stevvie." His smile grew. She hugged him lightly and grabbed his hand, leading him to the door, waving behind her for us to follow.

"Hey Namma-" Beck started to speak to her.

"Shut the fuck up!" she interrupted, whipping around and flipping him off again, her face momentarily shooting a scowl, then switching back to sweet before she turned.

I snickered and smiled at Beck, sticking out my tongue. As a response, he stuck his thumbs in his ears, palms out, and wiggled his fingers. He crossed his eyes, stuck out his tongue, blew raspberries, and spun around in little circles.

"You look plainly idiotic! Stop acting so childish!" Namma shoved her boot heel into his toes and pulled him down to her level by the collar of his shirt. "Now act like an adult! Right Jelli?" She glance-smiled at me before continuing back into the house.

He held his foot up and gawked at me. I stuck my tongue out again, which made him smile, then I followed Namma into her house.

Chasing after us, Beck picked me up by my waist and carried me into the kitchen. He spun me around and set me down in the doorway, wrapping his arms around me, he pulled me backward into a hug. We swayed side to side and watched as Namma made some soup for Stevvie. Beck was always a bit more comfortable here.

Namma grabbed two more bowls and stuck one in each of my hands. Whispering, so the kid couldn't hear,

"I've asked you two at least once a month -" she made direct eye contact with Beck. "For the last two years..." She put her hands on her hips ruffling her dress a bit. "When are you guys going to get together? When is my point going to get across?" Stevvie's head jerked up a little and some soup fell from his suddenly open mouth. He shook his head and went back to eating, this time leaning in to hear our conversation better.

"It's not-" I started to say.

"*We're not.*" Beck corrected for me. He grabbed a bowl from my grip, ducked around me and out of the hug.

The look on her face would've made you think we'd peed in her only cereal. Beck and I shrugged and shook our heads lightly with laughter. This just seemed to widen her eyes and further tighten the muscles in her jaw.

We sat about the old oak table eating, giggling, waiting for Namma to stop tapping her foot at us. Even Stevvie seemed to understand the joke, and he'd chosen our side, amused by her frustrations.

She sighed, rolled her eyes and walked to grab her own bowl, angry and annoyed at the whole lot of us. Every sip sounded like a growl, starting from deep within her and pouring out of her throat. The end of the table that she sat on erupted in an abnormally heavy sigh.

"Fine..." She smiled and shook her head. "Warning to you both though... I can *always* be more stubborn." She got up, cleaned her place at the table and without another word walked out, probably just to prepare more bedded cots, even though they were not needed.

Stevvie jumped down off his chair, following Namma's lead, and reached up to set his bowl in the sink. He toddled after her, asking if he could help with anything, and if she might have a bed for him as well.

Beck cleaned our dishes and went to turn on the lights I assumed. I went to get our bags from the front porch and set them in the doorway.

The entire left half of Namma's house was nearly empty, yet full of rows and rows of makeshift beds, sleeping bags and cots. A few beds held stragglers - none of which had joined us in our late meal - looking for a place to rest, but most were empty. The number of people that had been found had decreased greatly with each passing year. Gradually but surely, there were fewer of us out there, and the camps would likely soon collect the last.

Stevvie stumbled into the living room, dragging the bags behind him. I pulled mine and Beck's cots apart and helped the kid with the luggage.

Stevvie put his own bag down and stood staring at his cot, so happy that he looked as if he might cry. I tried not to ask about his past, about anyone's time before the Finish, but the question was burning in my brain... and so I asked.

"How long has it been since you've slept in a real bed? A bed just for you?" He didn't look at me. His small voice leaked quiet, sad words.

"Too long. Way too long..." I could feel the pain behind his words which surfaced as tears in his eyes. It was his past. Stevvie shook his head, then jumped on the bed, sighed out of joy, and fell limp as he succumbed to sleep.

"Too long..." Beck repeated, his voice distant. I turned and walked toward him to better hear what he had said. I was standing behind him when, over his shoulder, I saw the oh-so familiar blueberry keychain...

... About Two And A Half Years Earlier ...

"For me, really? Oh, thank you! Thank you!" Looking between the both of us, she jumped up off the ground and threw her arms around our necks. "I love it, thank you!"

She let go of us.

"You're nine now, and I was thinking..." Beck lightly squeezed my shoulder as he spoke, we shared a look. "*We* were thinking, you're responsible enough to start scavenging. If you want to, that is."

"Thank you, thank you! I do!" She squealed again, jumping and hugging us. When she pulled away, she swung the keychain from side to side in front of her. "Nine..."

... Present ...

"She loved blueberries so much..." He knew I too was staring at the keychain in his hand. Beck's voice told me he was also reliving the past as he turned to stand. He hugged me. He began to sob angrily into my shoulder and leaned his weight into me for support. "To long-"

"Much too long," I finished for him when his voice cracked and cut off. "Much too long..."

I took her death rough, with hundreds of sob-filled days, but Beck... he *died* that day. Right alongside her. Bleeding out onto the rocks and sand. He became an alcoholic within minutes. Even in a crowd or a conversation he was alone. Dark, cold grief like a noose, suffocated him and separated him from the world. He shattered like the pellets from the shell that killed her, both his hope and the bullet dusting the ground. I tried to find all of the pieces and put him back together, but I couldn't, and now I'm forced to watch as his cracked and hole-riddled-self cries, crumpled in my arms. Unable to do anything but hold him.

Neither of us truly healed.

The lights flickered above me, making my fear of the dark flare up, which then woke me. I rolled over, knowing the truth. *Even if they go out, there is enough light. I am safe.* I nearly had my eyes closed again before I noticed Beck was sitting up across from me, awake.

I let my eyelids fall and I took a deep breath, deciding whether or not I should engage him.

"Can't sleep?"

His head lifted some before dropping back down as he looked at his hands.

"Can. I'm just thinking." His back was to me and he was whispering, but his thick, sloppy western accent held strong. I assumed he wasn't thinking about her, because his voice didn't waver. I took that as a good sign.

"Try, alright?" I said. Almost in unison, we both leaned back and looked up to the ugly orange lights. The lights didn't flicker again, and the rest of the night was restful.

Stevvie woke me when he shook my arm.

"I can't reach the sink." He lifted up a toothbrush and a tube of toothpaste into my view. "Will you help me find a stool?"

I sighed and climbed out from under the covers.

"Let's go, then." His shy smile grew more confident. I knew where everything was in this house, so that journey ended rather quickly.

We stood at the sink, joking and splashing water at the cracked mirror.

"How'd you get to know Beck?" His words were nearly incomprehensible with the toothbrush hanging halfway from his mouth.

"I suppose we just did, over time, but that is long in the past. What about you? Your past?" I was curious, but rightfully cautious. I'd been avoiding this conversation since I met the boy. However, curiosity won me over.

His eyes widened and sharpened with fear, he looked as if he was searching for something that lingered in the air between him and the glass, perhaps something from the past.

"You don't have to tell me if you-"

He cut me off.

"I watched her die." He had found it, his reflection holding his glare. He found the memory. From how tightly he was squeezing the handle of his toothbrush, I could tell he despised the very thought of it.

"What?" Whispering, I stepped closer and crouched down. "Who died?"

"My mommy."

I almost said something more, but I was pulled into his emotions, the pain in his next words.

"The only family I can remember, screaming in pain and anger at me. Threatening to kill me, if only she could get the chance - no, more like promising. When stage three hit... she couldn't even get a full apology out. She hit the ground, twitching and spitting that *darkness*."

"She was infected for weeks, and there was nothing I could do!" He was screaming now, coupled by slamming his fists into the counter repeatedly. "She just sat there and pulled against the chains. Cussing at me every time that I cried. I knew it wasn't her saying all those horrible things, but it hurt so much..."

I pulled him into a hug to quiet him and to comfort him. I lifted him up, both of us were crying loudly, and I cradled his head in my hand.

Beck grabbed my arm, and with that pulled us both into his arms.

"I heard it all..." He kissed me on the top of my head. Then he forced eye contact, his eyes were so angry and serious that it began to scare me.

"He should *not* have gone through that. No one should."

We all stood there. The silence was so sharp it could have cut. The kid cleared his throat, attempting to break the awkward emptiness around us. He was unsuccessful.

"What's with the... weird?" Namma said, waving her hand in front of her face to brush away some gray hairs. Beck gave her an angry glance.

"Oh, I didn't know that I ordered a side of death glare. You'll have to send it back to the kitchen and tell the chef to reimburse me for my troubles." Namma wasn't big on jokes or sarcasm, but every time she made a comment like that, it always cheered up Beck. Even now it worked some.

As if on cue, he smiled and rolled his eyes, setting aside this inevitable conversation.

"He wants to apologize for the inconvenience and wonders if free dessert will satisfy his most loyal customer. Will it?" One of his eyebrows rose to leave the other.

"Hell yes!" Namma screeched and jumped at her victory. "We're having dessert!" She was nearly singing and dancing as she left the hall.

Silence almost set in before Stevvie asked.

"What is dessert?"

Beck's smile twisted into something wicked. He shrugged and walked out, moving from wall to wall, as if he were hiding in an old spy movie.

"You'll never know..." He yelled once he was out of sight. "Never know..." The second half was part whisper and part giggle.

"It's sweet, and you'll love it," I said when I noticed the light worry beginning to weigh on the kid's face. His expression softened, but was still cautious. He grabbed the stool and dragged it behind him.

"Do you think I could watch?" his little voice called after Beck.

"How 'bout you help? I could always use some."

Stirring and stirring, the boys sat on the counter and cooked, laughing and having fun as they did. On occasion Beck would look my way and his smile would widen. Namma joined me in the doorway to watch, as Stevvie slid the dented pans onto the wood-burning stove.

... About Four Years Ago ...

I turned the corner, my vision blocked by the many boxes I was carrying. I couldn't see the idiot running from a hoard of torturous toddlers. He collided with me, boxes and blankets falling everywhere around us.

He fell on me, elbowing me hard in the ribs and leaving me at a loss of breath-needing insults.

"Not a good first impression," he stated, smiling almost clumsily at me.

"Except on my ribs..." I said quietly, rubbing them after catching my breath. He blushed, embarrassed at my words. I tried to roll out from under him, but he stuck a hand over my mouth. He tilted his head, listening for something after a small noise caught his attention. I shifted quietly and he moved his hand off my mouth and in front of his in a shushing motion.

A few long seconds of silence passed before he let out a sigh of relief. Some toddlers wobbled around the corner. He moaned something angrily in a response to them, then rolled away from me and into a seated position. The kids rushed over to him. One went around him and hugged him around his neck, and the others sat on his knees and on the dirt around him.

"Fine..." he groaned. He shrugged at me, *what can you do?* it seemed to say. "They jumped onto the deck!" he shouted, throwing his arms to the sky, startling the kids before they leaned ever closer with great interest. "Not knowing if it is for peace, or war..." He lowered his head, and the kids did the same. "They drew their swords for good measure, and the battle ignited like the powder from the others' guns. Who will win? No one knows for sure."

The kids all lingered in suspense, but he shook his head, "No more."

"That's not long enough... you said if we caught up to you, we'd get to hear how it ends!" The kid around his neck wined in his ear.

"That *is* how it ends... but I might tell y'all more when camp dinner is over," he said, pulling the kids off of him and standing up. "Until then, y'all need to get home." the kids voiced their complaints but scurried off to their worrying parents, nonetheless.

He walked over to me and started picking up my things. At this point I hadn't even attempted to pick anything up. I was still trying to wrap my head around what I had just witnessed. He stood over the side of me, one hand full of boxes and the other outstretched in my direction to offer assistance. This only reminded me that I was still laying on the dirty ground.

"They just won't get that I have to make the stories up - and it's hard work, too," he said, after helping me to my feet. Still carrying my stuff, he walked with me to my temporary residence.

"Then why do you do it?"

"They need it. They shouldn't have to worry about real monsters. They shouldn't have to really fear the dark. But in full honesty... I need it just as much, maybe more... their joy keeps me from going crazy from the reality of... well, reality. That's why I tell them tales with happy endings: to make them want to fight for theirs."

I spoke, slowing my pace to a near stop.

"This is it." I gestured to the broken building we stood in front of. He handed me my boxes.

"I think it's sweet, what you do for them." I looked back over my shoulder in a sort of goodbye. He turned in his walking, smiled, nodded, and finished crossing the street. He went over one house to the left and walked into it, and I could just make out the sound of children tackling him yet again.

I laughed aloud to myself and dropped my stuff in the entryway. I wandered from room to room, exploring the house. It was extremely small and worn down, but it was also only temporary. Eventually, the town would tear it down and replace it with a garage-sized concrete cube, at least, that is what I had heard. Then someone else's life would fill its walls. But for now it was my turn.

This time *he* was holding boxes and running, nearly crashing into me, again, at the camp dinner.

"Sorry to bump into you like this," he said. He couldn't stop bouncing and scanning the area frantically. "But could you hide me?"

Without thinking I ushered him behind a row of large pillars that held up the pavilion ceiling.

"Why are you hiding?" I whispered over my shoulder as I tried to casually lean on the pillar's side opposite to him.

"My life is at stake." His voice quivered with fear. "The little monsters, they're out for *blood*." The last word caught sharp and raspy in his throat.

"Those sweet little angels?" I asked. He scoffed at me as I continued. "What could they do?"

"You'd be surprised..." he said. His voice trailed off in thought, followed by a full-body shudder. The kids ran in front of me. Once they were safely past us he whimpered quietly.

"Why are the 'monsters' after you?"

"These..." He reached his arm around the stone structure and handed me a ball of squishy blue goo. "They're my *second* specialty."

"What is it?" I rolled the ball over in my hand, examining it.

"Delicious. Eat it quickly before one of those *demons* sees it."

I couldn't place why, but something about this man made me feel like I could trust him.

I cautiously set the thing in my mouth. *Cake?* I bit down, quickly overwhelmed by the smooth liquid texture and the sweet yet tart flavor. The taste buzzed in my mouth long after I swallowed.

"Thoughts?" he asked with surety and confidence. Clearly, he already knew the answer.

"That..." I said, dragging out the pause longer than necessary. "Was, beyond all shadow of a doubt, the best dessert I have *ever* eaten!"

"I'm glad." At the compliment his voice softened out of its previous cockiness. His smile as well, though I couldn't see it, it was clear in his tone.

The kids circled around the facility again, apparently running a long loop. They came up behind us and tackled him. As a defense, he lifted his arms above his head, out of reach of their grubby, thieving hands. They, as a counter, tickled him to the ground and stole his boxes of blueberry sweets. I nearly went after them, but he waved me off and waited in silence.

When the last of their screams faded, he sighed.

"Finally, they're gone." Still on the ground, he rolled over onto his elbows and pulled a small box out of his jacket pocket. He waved through the air, then tapped the ground in front of him, sitting up into a legs-crossed position. "Come. I'll share." He saw my slight hesitancy and added, "I don't bite. Promise." He scooted back to give me more space.

We sat and joked about nothing in particular. When we were done, I walked him home and I watched the sun set alone from my house. I put the sweets he had given me in a box, though I didn't know how well they would keep.

I took one last look through my window, out at all those lights. *So many lights...* and it hit me like a rock to the head... *I don't know this stranger's name.*

... Present ...

Beck took off his over-shirt and folded it into a lopsided rectangle. He used it to pull the pans out of the flames. Stevvie climbed onto the counter and leaned over the pans to get a better look. Beck slid him back, not wanting him to get burned.

I snuck behind Beck while he was busy holding Stevvie back. I reached around him and grabbed one of the treats. It was hot and made me yelp as I tossed it between my hands.

"What're you doing?" he demanded as he whipped around, still using one hand to hold Stevvie at a safe distance. I moved my hands closer to my face. "Don't!" he said. "Don't..." I put it in my mouth anyway, the heat burned my tongue, and I spat the treat out immediately. The temperature surprised me more than it should have, and I shrieked, fanning at my mouth.

He slid over to my side and opened my mouth, looking in it as if he was checking me for strep. He stood back and rolled his eyes at me.

"You need to be more careful, Jelli." He scolded sternly.

A loud, high-pitched scream forced all of our heads to turn. Stevvie was holding his right hand close to his chest. I ran to him, closely followed by Beck and Namma.

At first I had thought he'd burned his hand on the pans, but then I saw the fresh blood pooling over the older stains on his once white shirt. I pulled him into a hug and ran to the bathroom, ordering Beck to get a first aid kit.

I set Stevvie on the counter and grabbed his hand. He tried to resist. I turned on the water.

"I need to clean your hand, but it *will* hurt." I spoke calmly to him.

"No!" he yelled, his tears falling faster. I stuck his hand under the sputtering faucet. It faded a clearer red when I pried his fingers open. He sobbed and tried to pull against me, but I held him tightly and refused to budge.

Beck ran into the bathroom with a box of first aid supplies, closing the door behind him to block the view of gathering onlookers. Shutting out those drawn by the noise, he shifted his attention to us.

"Stitches?" he asked, opening the box. I looked at the deep cut and nodded somberly.

He sighed and took my spot at Stevvie's side. I began to pace. Beck whispered something to him that I couldn't hear, and his cries softened as he nodded. Beck folded a rag, and Stevvie bit down on it. Beck started pouring hydrogen peroxide on the boy's hand to sterilize it, making his cries build up again.

"Okay, now's the time. Close your eyes, and don't open them 'til I say." The kid obeyed. "It's sunny," Beck said, making the first stitch. "And warm." He spoke slowly and calmly, talking his way through one stitch at a time.

He continued walking Stevvie through this beautiful paradise to distract him from the stabbing needle and the strings. It had been a long time since I'd heard him tell his stories. Over two years. When he finished the stitches, and Stevvie ran out of tears, Beck ended his story and wrapped the wound in gauze.

"You can open your eyes now," Beck said, waving to stop my obsessive walking and wiping the still wet tears off of the kid's cheeks. Stevvie wrapped his arms around Beck's neck, and Beck motioned me over. I was hesitant to ruin their moment, but joined in on their hug.

"What hour is it?" My head shot up. *Crap, we've gotta run...* "Gather the stragglers who want to go. I'll get our stuff packed," I said to Beck, and he nodded. "Namma, watch Stevvie, we've got to get going," I yelled to her, out the now-opened-by-Beck door.

Namma came around the corner holding a bloody knife. "Was propped up on a cutting board, kid mustn't have seen it and set his hand down too fast, and..." She tilted the knife and made a clicking noise with her tongue.

After turning off the water, I pulled the knife out of her hand and lightly tossed it in the bathroom sink. I picked the kid off the counter and gently handed him to Namma, smiling and mouthing my thanks. She nodded in return. I rushed off to the back of the house and started packing our bags. While Beck jogged from room to room, making sure everyone who wanted to leave was awake and ready to run, I did my best to rapidly gather what we had brought.

    We met up at the front of the house as the sun topped the hills. Namma handed me a small box, setting down Stevvie after I had handed the boys all of their bags. We stepped out onto the porch as the last of the strangers caught up with us. I glanced back and counted heads. All ten of us would leave the safety and comfort of Namma's house.

Day Two

We took our first steps of the travels of the second day, rushed and all but behind schedule. That buzz of knowing that each step drew us closer to The Camp - one day closer to safety - ran deeply in the majority of us: Mostly Stevvie and the few others who hadn't seen it yet, but we all felt it dancing in the air.

The weather today was more agreeable and less like the sun wanted us all to burn alive. Scattered clouds created a simple shade. *It'll rain soon, I know it*. Beck must have been thinking the same thing. I could tell as our gazes fell from the glowing clouds to meet up. We nodded and both waved at the others to follow. *We have a long day of walking ahead of us.*

I carried two backpacks and Stevvie's duffle. His hand was hurting too much to stabilize the weight. Some other people in the group broke the general unspoken rule of 'no more than two bags' but I understood where they were coming from. They were moving their entire lives. Even in the Finish, that takes some space, so I let it slide, unmentioned.

The ten of us were naturally distanced by our individual walking speeds throughout the several hours we'd walked since Namma's house. Beck and I led the trek, well ahead the others as a faint halt at the back of the pack stretched us more, something drifting farther from the back of the pack.

Beck rolled his eyes and sighed. His head rolled back, gaze drifting my way, searching for eye contact. *How is he so good at begging?* I raised my eyebrows and tilted my head downward in protest, not breaking the contact. He tilted his head in response, scrunched his brows, stuck out his lower lip, and batted his eyelashes. His undeniable 'puppy face'.

I let out a sigh.

"Fine."

His victory smile forced my eyes to roll. I walked away from him and Stevvie high-fiving, passing through small clusters of tired faces. I got to the back of the group and was greeted by a man helping someone onto a rock to sit.

"Hello. I'm Daultin and this is my wife, Prince." He leaned forward and shook my hand, then led me to the woman on the rock. She smiled widely and shook my hand as well. I casually wiped the sweat from my palm onto my jeans, halting the action as I noticed the obvious. She was pregnant. *Very* pregnant.

I pressed my palm against my forehead, my irritation and stress rising. A quick, quiet growl slipped through my lips, stopped by sucking in a deep breath just a moment before it was too late. I forced a closed-mouth smile and shifted my weight, walking a few passes back. I needed to make some space to think of a solution.

"Beck, you're going to want to see this..." I decided, hollering at him over my shoulder.

He jogged up, stopping and looking at me.

"Ya?" I pointed with a twitch of my head and a side glance to the couple. The man handed his wife a water bottle before stepping out of view.

"Oh,- crap!" Beck whispered to himself. He sighed and looked at me for answers. "Plan?" He mouthed. I shrugged, making him run a hand through his hair.

With several more hours of laborious walking and limited, unintentional shade ahead of us, I was frustrated too and wanted to cuss. The baby might not make it, and we all knew that.

It was early... They were in a different room... I dug through my thoughts to come up with a reason to not notice such an obviously pregnant woman in the group as I made my way to the couple.

"I've got it." I mouthed to Beck. He was chewing his lip, an infrequent nervous habit of his.

I nodded to the husband and he took a step back. *We will just have to walk.*

"Prince, is it?" She nodded. "Can I?" I gestured to the rock and she scooted over. "How far along are you?"

"Eight months," She cupped her hands around her large stomach and straightened her back in a little stretch. I smiled and bit my tongue, trying to come up with more to talk about.

"I know a really good doctor at The Camp. I can introduce you, when we get there, if you would like?"

She smiled.

"Thank you, that would be great. I am kind of freaking out here." She and her husband shared a sad, worried look.

I nodded.

"...But," She frowned. "We need to get to the next stop safely, first." She sighed and took a long drink of water. Her grip on the bottle was so tight that her knuckles went white.

"Do you think you can walk?" I asked. Another glance passed between the couple.

She took a deep breath and nodded to her husband, who then helped her off of the rock. He held her weight while she got her balance, then she looked at me and smiled a little. The large amounts of sweat that laced her skin, shimmered in the sun.

I crossed my fingers behind my back in an attempt to gather luck, and Beck walked to my side. I felt his fingers uncross mine. He held my hand and squeezed it tightly, to comfort me.

... About Two and a Half Years Ago ...

It was warm and sunny. That day's wind brushed through the cattail and rippled the surface of the water. She moved her leg for balance, but played it off as the wind that disturbed the pond, the fish believed it.

She drove the staff into the water, parting the murky parts of the pond and replacing the green-gray with red. She pulled the carved stick out of the pond and waved it above her head, she waved it to Beck and myself. The fish at the end sparkled in the high light of the sun.

Beck slid the knife down the fish's stomach with a certainty that was honestly somewhat unsettling. The little girl set her hands on the counter and lifted herself, tippy toeing to try and see. Beck set his elbow on the top of her head and pushed her down out of view, and he continued to gut the fish.

He slid the cut up fish on a pan and seasoned it with what he had, setting a sliced lemon, which had cost him more than he would say, on top of it before placing it into the wood burner. She sat with a wide smile on her face in front of its closed door and waited for it to finish cooking.

... Present ...

Prince's walking was stunted at best, even with Daultin's help. As our group moved I realized something: we all seemed to realize it. *We might not make it before dark. We might all die tonight.* I looked at the back of Beck's head, the thought twisted my stomach with how much I wanted him to turn and see it in my eyes, and acknowledge it.

Stevvie saw it, the empty sand in all directions, the fear in my eyes and our overly slowed pace. He looked at me and waited until I returned the action of his staring. His eyes were young, but the innocence was shrouded if not entirely dead. He knew what would happen; he had seen it before. Those eyes said it all.

The sky was orange and pink. Barely any of the sun was still visible, but it was just bright enough - just enough time - to make it to the darkened silhouette of a house in the distance. The *darkened* silhouette...

I looked at Beck and the understanding clicked painfully. His posture went rigid, and he began to run. He dropped his bags and simply ran. I raised my hand to stop the others from following his lead, even though it took everything in me to not follow him myself.

The windows were dark. The people inside were probably dead. *It's a waste for Beck to check.*

Our speed was unintentionally increased, until the entire group was doing their best to run. Beck tried to open the door, but it was locked. He pounded his open palm against the wood, unrelenting. We reached the porch just as the handle twisted.

A tall, skinny and ghostly pale man opened the door. He scanned our faces individually. He was looking for the darkness. He leaned farther out the door frame and looked to the mountains, blurred in the distance by the heat and shifting light. With one shaky nod he moved to let us in.

It was a small house, and empty enough that a tumble weed would have seemed strange and out of place. The house had a very simple design and an eerie feeling to it. A mixture of dust and silence in the air made the hair on the back of my neck stand up. I slowed my speed, pretending to examine the space of the rooms, but I was really just trying to distance myself from the tall man.

We reached the back of the house and walked through a doorway to a small, barely lit room. The tall man ducked to enter, and with his deep voice explained their situation.

"We've all been stuck in this house for four days." He cleared his throat. "We ran out of food on the first day, water on the third." Someone coughed and winced at the effort it took. "We would leave, but none of us have been to The Camp, and none of us know the way."

"I do. We'll get going in the morning, but for now, we need to get some lights on." Beck said as he looked at the sad half circle of puddled candles and the dim flashlight hanging in the corner. I reached in his backpack, tossed the four new strangers a couple of flashlights, then handed Beck his bag and dug through mine to get some more.

We started hanging the flashlights on the many small hooks coming down from the ceiling. They had been installed long before my first visit here.

... One Week Ago ...

The boy and I walked to what was once Main Street where we found a relatively untouched gas station. He tried to open the door, but wasn't successful. I tried and failed as well, and he looked at me with a look like, 'I could have told you it was locked'. He smiled and picked up a sturdy rock, tossing it between his hands before he threw it through the glass.

I flinched and exhaled a laugh. Nodding, I pulled down my sleeve, reached through the newly formed hole in the glass, and unlocked the door. I pulled my hand out, swung the door open, and gestured with my other arm for him to enter first.

He skipped into the gas station and began wandering the dusty aisles. He gawked, looking around at the common - mostly unknown to him - wonders that the shelves held.

I walked to the back. On a mission, on the clock. I jumped the counter, knocking some things over in the process, which temporarily caught the boy's attention, and I hurried to the office. I scanned the walls and found my target: an electrical box. I followed the written instructions, but got no light. *I'll have to improvise.*

I walked back out of the office and looked through the aisles, scanning for the boy as well. I found him and ushered him to me. I reached into one of my bags and pulled out two flashlights. I clicked them on and lifted him up so he could reach to hang them using the burnt-out ceiling lights.

We watched as the light faded outside, until all was dark except our little circle in a rundown store. To fill the time, we talked.

"So, kid, what's your name? I think calling you 'kid' is gonna get old, pretty fast."

"My name is Stevenson. Stevenson Hunts," he said, beaming with pride.

"Okay... so what's your Finish name?" I asked.

"Finish name? What's a 'Finish'?" His face twisted with confusion.

I let out a light chuckle and bit my tongue, trying to find the right words to explain... well, all of it. I took a deep breath and just started talking.

"You know about the darkness, and its- well, we call it the Finish." He nodded. "A lot of people don't know how to deal with it, not alone, the way it is. There's this place these people built. We call it 'The Camp'. It serves as a sort of refuge for those who are lost and in need of help." He nodded again, just taking in the information. "These people, they come to this place with scars - " He tilted his head. "Um, they're hurt, in their hearts and their minds, they're scared. They want to disconnect from their past, so they come up with names. These new names usually have some connection to their birth names, but they represent the new them, the surviving them."

"So, I get to pick a name that I like, that I want people to know me by?" I nodded and he smiled at that. "How do I pick one I'll like?"

"Pick one that shows your personality."

"Okay. What's your Finish name?"

"It's Jelli, with an 'I'." I replied.

"Why'd you choose Jelli?" he asked, adding to the list of questions for me to answer.

"'Cause I make really good jelly, and my birth name started with an 'I'. So, Jelli." He sat in deep contemplation before I offered a question of my own. "Do you do stuff like that a lot?" I said, gesturing to the broken glass at the front door. He smiled and nodded, but his face went flat when he noticed my glance at the blood on his shirt, and he looked to the ground.

"So you're young, but very grown up?" I moved the subject along. "How about the name of someone else, like a bold character?"

"I saw on an old TV once. There was a baby, but he acted older than he was."

"That could work, just put your own twist on it somehow." His face lit up with joy, as if he'd been called by - and replied to - the name he was thinking of a thousand plus times.

"Stevvie? Stevvie." He repeated it many times over, getting a feel for his new name and growing confidence in it. "I love it!"

After a few minutes of him asking me to call him by his Finish name and then having him replying as if he was surprised, he asked me a new question.

"Are *you* going to this camp thing?" The question really did catch me off guard, I had to think a moment before answering.

"Um, yeah? I am."

"Is it a good place?"

"The best we could do. It's definitely better than *this*." I lifted my arms, meaning to point to the entire dying world.

"Can I go?" It seemed more like a plea than a question as his eyes begged for a way out of whatever nightmares he'd been living through until now.

"I guess, why not? It's several days of walking. Can you make it that far?"

"'Course I can make it that far, I'm Stevvie!" he said, smiling at both the use of his new name and the thought of seeing The Camp. He started shivering, so I handed him the smallest of the few jackets that I had in my bag. It drowned him, but at very least it kept him warm and covered up the blood.

When the sun rose again I grabbed some supplies, then I woke the kid. He just couldn't stay awake for as much of the night as I could, in spite of how hard he tried.

... Present ...

A sudden, heavy banging on the basement door caught everyone's attention. Making the four new travelers cower in fear. They shrank into the corners, not even thinking of the light. One of them violently sobbed and wailed in another language.

All eyes on the door as the hinges, one by one, loosened and fell to the ground. At the second to last pin drop, Beck popped the question hot on all of our minds.

"What is behind that door?" The lack of answers forced him to pull his focus off the now violently bending door and scream the questions again.

The tall man answered.

"Our guide- he's infected."

The door hit the ground only seconds before the man. He fell face first. A pool of blood grew from under him, first red, then black. Black as the darkness of his eyes. Though none of us could see them, we knew what they looked like.

The moment passed so quickly that the effects of the gun's noise had a bit of a delay.

We saw the shot, the kid and I, but Beck felt it. Beck's eyes filled with the rush of adrenaline from the kill, from every kill. In that moment it was clear that he knew the power of the slightest twitch of his finger. You could almost watch all of his slaughters cross his mind, even *hers*.

"Someone tell me what the hell is going on here. Why did I have to shoot your guide in the head?" He turned to us after putting away his gun. "And someone please get that girl to shut up," he said, pointing to the woman still screaming away in her own little world of tears.

He took a sheet that someone had pulled from their bag and laid it over the body. He pulled some dried food - which we found with the sheet - and passed it out to the hungry.

The travelers explained the story of how they got in this situation, it went something like this...

They had just arrived at the stop nearest to The Camp, running low on their supplies. They were doing well enough, though, and had gotten halfway through the night smoothly, when their guide thought he heard something in the basement.

He went downstairs to check, but he had been doing renovations and had no built-in lights down there. His flashlight blew, and the darkness infected him. The people had no choice but to lock the door, not knowing that most of their supplies were in the dark with the now dying madman.

He had picked up the only thing he could think of and began to hack at the electrical box. He broke his only real weapon, an ax, in the process and wasn't able to use it to escape the basement. It was a race against time itself, time and luck. Four people, one maniac, and a group of slow-walking strangers.

The night went on, filled with introductions and more stories, but exhaustion got the best of me. I slept slumped against a wall for the majority of the night, along with Stevvie and Prince. Daultin sat at Prince's side, Stevvie in a corner near us, and Beck sat by me. All night, he listened to the others' stories, holding my hand. He stayed awake and protected me, he knew how much the darkness bothered me.

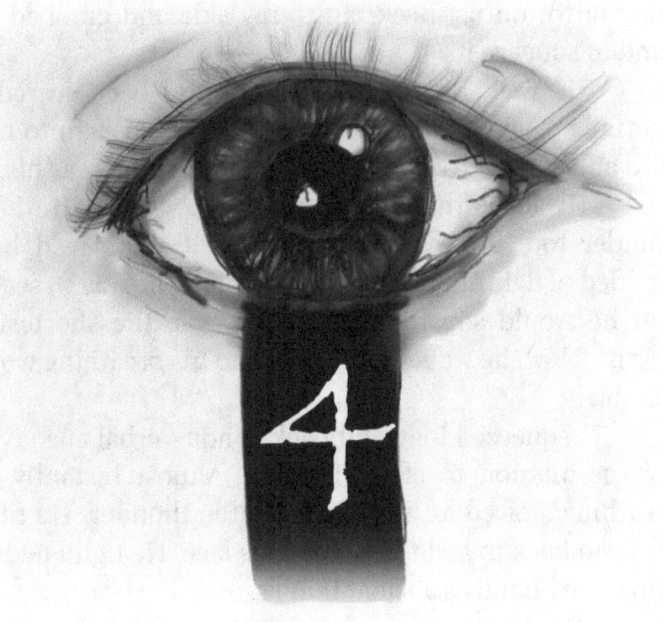

The Camp

Morning came and the fourteen of us left. One more day and we'd all see The Camp, some of us for the first time.

As we had guessed the day before, it rained. It was refreshing at first, but as most things have multiple truths, this sweet thing soon turned sour. The rain was amazing, but quickly the mud began to slow our pace.

As some parts of old houses started to form out of the watered-down sand and rubble, we saw it standing sturdy on the horizon, its light blaring against the darkened, cloudy background... The Camp.

We were soaked to the bone. The passing of time was hard to measure with the thick clouds, yet we dredged onward. Lightning lit up the skies, joined by a thunderous cracking sound as if the skies were spitting to let the water flood down on us. Beck ran to my side and grabbed my hand to squeeze it.

He was shivering, he had always been scared of lightning, as far as I knew. Everyone has the right to hold onto at least one irrational childhood fear, this was his.

He loves the rain, as many people do. He loves thunder too, but ever since he was a child, he'd been terrified of lightning. When he was small, he was so scared that he would sob for hours after even the shortest of storms. Now, he would just shake and his breathing would tremble.

I squeezed his hand back, a non-verbal cue giving him permission to close his eyes. Almost instantly his breathing slowed as he listened to the thunder. He tilted his head back to feel the rain on his face. He tightened his grip on my hand as a silent thanks.

The lightning ran for only a small portion of the storm, but for Beck and I it felt like hours. The rain, on the other hand, showed no signs of lifting or slowing.

As we walked on, the lights in the distance grew brighter. The Camp wasn't fully powered, but it strongly pulled itself off of the background of the sky. It was from the cage-protected electric lights, bouncing from the thick, gray walls of The Camp.

The Camp with its many high, concrete walls lined with barbed wire, providing protection to its few hundred residents. People who were once strangers crammed into makeshift homes together. Every house in the camp was covered with some source of light or another. No deep shadows were possible even in the darkest of nights, inside those walls.

Ours isn't the original. There are hundreds of camps, thousands maybe, ours is only the seventy first Camp of the North American region. Every continent calls its own region and every region names or numbers however they please. The Camps attempted to make contact with each other once, but the radios went silent not long after the start of the Finish.

I walked to the wall, it was really a magnificent sight as it towered over us, and Beck nodded up to the guards to allow everyone in. They filed in, but I stayed behind. I pulled my hand out of my pocket and walked to the edge of the wall as the last few people wandered in. I set my hand down on the smooth stone and began to run, dragging my hand along the wall as I went.

I got to the entrance, still in a full run, when suddenly I was no longer on the ground. Beck had jumped out from behind the frame of the entrance, lifted me in the air and spun me around. It caught me off guard and I had to hold onto his shoulders for balance. He set me down soon after picking me up and I couldn't help but laugh lightly. He looked at me, and his smile grew softer as he kissed my forehead.

I stopped laughing and my jaw fell agape when he did this. He turned to cover a slight blush that was growing on his face and waved for me to follow him into The Camp.

"You coming?" he asked me without turning.

... About Four Years Ago ...

It was early enough in the morning for the lights to still be on, but I was awake. The heavy knocking on the front door floated in through the slightly open window near it. I rolled my eyes and stumbled out of bed, sleep clouded my eyes as I walked. I grumbled nonsense to myself after I nearly fell down the stairs. *Watch where you walk.* I thought to myself as I planted my feet beneath me.

I pressed my forehead on the surprisingly soothing, hard wood of the door and began to drift off to sleep, before the loud knocking returned to ruin my slumber.

"Who's there?" I hollered through the door, not lifting my head, but letting it sway to the side.

"Oh, come on... you can't have forgotten me that quickly..." The stranger's muffled voice pushed its way through the wood.

My head fell from the door to its frame, and I swung it open.

"Why're you here? What do you want?" I turned my head and lifted it slightly to look at him.

"Good morning to you, too." he said, inviting himself inside and tilting his head like mine to make more direct eye contact. "So, you're one of the newest members to join The Camp. It's very nice to meet you."

"We've met before," I said, trying to stand without the help of a wall and without allowing sleep to pull me to the floor.

He smiled in response to my grumpy attitude and replied.

"Well yes, we have. Not enough to know you, though, and apparently, you're *not* a morning person." I rolled my eyes, and he gave a toothy smile at the action. "I have a request. Well, more like a favor."

"Tell me what it is, *then* I'll decide if I'm awake enough to strangle you or just do you a favor," I said, only half joking.

He let out a laugh.

"Works for me. So... let me take you on a date - to make up for *literally* running into you." He couldn't hide his nervousness, he kept shifting his weight side to side as if it would kill him to hold still; his hands fidgeted away in spite of his efforts to still them.

"I barely know you. How do I know you're not, like, a murderer?" I joked again.

"Cross my heart and swear, I'm *not* a murderer. I'm not even *that* weird or creepy," he said, drawing an 'x' over his chest with a finger.

I sat there a while, mulling over whether or not to agree.

"Okay. When is it?"

He looked at his watch for a moment before answering me.

"However long it would take you to get ready." I eyed him and he nodded with a light, cheesy smile. He pointed to the stairs and leaned against the now closed door.

I rolled my eyes and ran up the stairs. I paused for a moment in the middle of the staircase to tell him, "I'll be down in fifteen minutes."

"It's casual," he shouted after me.

"Five, then."

He walked me through the streets, telling me not to look. I was untrusting, but closed my eyes anyway. After what felt like an hour, but probably wasn't, he stopped walking and let go of my hand. He stepped to my side and told me that it was okay for me to open my eyes.

"It's a wall...?" I questioned him, looking at the stone corner.

"Yep." He nodded, quite proud of himself. "Don't worry, I'll get you breakfast afterwards. But..." He gestured to the wall in response to my confusion. "Just, run."

His eyes rolled a little as I seemed to grow even more suspicious of the situation. He took my hand and walked me to the wall, setting our hands together on the cool stone. "Now run. It's fun. Just make sure not to push too hard, or you'll shred up your fingertips."

I started to walk, and he sighed.

"I know it sounds crazy and a little childish, but just trust me. You'll like it, *because* it's a little childish - everyone needs to be spontaneous every now and again." I sighed and began to run.

It *was* fun. It *was* childish. It hurt my hand, but I *did* enjoy it. We ran half the length of the wall before we fell to the ground, laughing and coughing for air. He leaned over and quickly kissed me on the cheek, I froze in place and blushed against my will. We laid like that under the sun, in that comfortable silence for a while. The way that the light hit his brown eyes made them look like pools of caramel, so very sweet to look at. Too soon we stood up and walked back into The Camp to find some place to get breakfast.

As we walked, I mentioned a thought that weighed heavily on my mind. "We're on a date, but we don't even know each other's names. So, what is your name?"

"Tell me yours first, mystery mistress," he demanded.

"Isabelle. You?"

"Ethan, but my Finish name is Beck Shot."

I looked at him like he was crazy and asked him what that was. Then he explained to me how people get to pick a new name to leave their old lives behind. And I picked mine. I chose 'Jelli'.

... Present ...

"Yeah, I'm coming." I took one last look at the wall, reminiscing about our first date. Then I followed the group and Beck into The Camp.

As we walked through the entrance the people's jaws dragged on the packed dirt. Their breathing was deep and loud with clear awe, it was like that for all but Beck and me. We stood about in awe at the fact that none of the people in our group had entered any camp like this until now. *An entire run of newcomers, that's a rare sight these days.*

Stevvie stopped his gawking to turn towards Beck and myself, and the kid let out a long sigh and turned again, this time to gesture to the world ahead. His arms spread widely to his future life, the somewhat unfinished stone structures and old townhomes that littered the space.

I cleared my throat and glanced at Beck as a way to tell him I would take over with the introductions this time.

"Now, everyone, if you'll follow me, we'll start the tour with a good meal, fresh water and registration." My voice brought the people out of their dazed states, and we started the walk to the front right corner of the camp where the school was.

Some of the residents had decided early on to use the elementary school in the corner of the camp rather than trying to tear it down. Its purposes varied for what people needed. Most commonly it stood as a school, a home for orphaned children, a dinning hall and a public medical facility.

We walked to the cafeteria, and fell in line for fresh, hot gruel and some clean water. At the end of the line, Daultin sped up to stand at my side. Like me he was holding two trays. We walked together to sit with a few others from our group and handed out the extra trays. We sat by Stevvie who beamed and quickly stuffed the food into his tired face.

"Are you sure about this doctor? I don't mean to seem rude, we just want to be safe." Prince said. Her husband took her hand.

"Oh, no I understand completely. He is trustworthy and very qualified. He has been taking care of this camp for years, and has even taken care of a few of the pregnant women here. You'll be in good hands." They simultaneously let out small sighs of relief before beginning to chat quietly amongst themselves.

Under the table Beck, who sat next to me, grabbed my hand. I stole a quick glance at him and saw the pain behind the mask of his smile. It was similar to the pain I felt from his tight, shaky grip.

... About Three Years Ago ...

Beck looked nervous, wringing his hands tightly and shifting his weight on the chair.

"Something wrong?" I asked.

"No," he nearly shouted, lifting and shaking his hands at me. "I - I uh..." He swallowed loudly. "I uh - I want to have kids." He stumbled over the words as they ran out of his mouth.

"Oh." The single word was dull, yet so full of emotion and surprise. It came out as a monotonous knife to his chest.

"Not *right this second*, but eventually -" I fell into the chair across from him and my hand rose to silence him. "I can't have kids - I want to, but I *can't*." I couldn't move my eyes to meet his, couldn't take them off my hands which I folded on the table. Beck leaned forward, lifted the knot of my hands and kissed them once. My gaze, with great resistance, followed the air to meet his teary eyes. He gave me a sad, fake smile and a singular, understanding nod.

... Present ...

He gave my hand one last knuckle whitening squeeze before going back to his food.

"If you two want to come with us after being placed in a house, we could introduce you to him today." My suggestion was immediately answered by nods. Hopefully this was one of De's more sane days, and he would play nice to make a good first impression.

The group gradually finished eating and joined us in our waiting outside of the school's double doors. Beck called the attention back to the tour by clearing his throat. We walked along the left wall and explained the living placements and house-grouping system.

We walked to the back of the camp, and as we passed the farms, we talked about some of our planting, rotation and irrigation plans.

"Everyone needs to do a job, find your skills and put them to good use. For The Camp to support the numbers we have, we need workers," Beck said to the group when we reached the back right corner. "Hell, even watching the water helps." He gestured to some people working on the part of the river that ran under The Camp's walls. His lighter, joking tone caused some chuckles to rise from the people.

We walked around and passed the last few rows of houses to finish our tour, and we arrived once again at the school.

"Go to the main office, answer some questions, and get placed in a house. We'll let you get settled for a few days, then you'll need to find some form of work that fits you." They all agreed in their own ways and stood there, staring at Beck. "Well, go. Start your lives," he said, waving them away and toward the school.

I stopped Prince and Daultin, told them to meet us here at the school after they put their things inside.

... About Four Years Ago ...

I sat in the child-sized chair talking to the lady behind the counter.

"How many people?" I raised my eyebrows, stared blankly and she repeated the question. "How many people are you traveling with?"

"Uh, traveling? None, it's just me."

"We have the space. Would you like to live in a house alone?"

"Since there's space, yeah, sure." She nodded and scribbled down something onto a plastic sheet protector that was over a map of The Camp.

"Here," she said, spinning the map and handing me a slip of paper with a letter and some numbers written on it. "You're here, and your house is here." She pointed to the map twice. "Can you find it yourself, or would you like me to get someone to help you?"

"I can probably find it myself. Thanks though."

"Would you like me to get someone to help you carry your supplies?"

"No thank you, I'm fine." I didn't want to seem rude, but I was still trying to get used to there being so many people around... non infected people that is.

"Well, if you can't find it or simply change your mind, just come back here and say so. Okay?"

... Present ...

Stevvie had calmed down enough from the day's events to walk normally. However, the beaming smile on his face refused to subside.

"So, your thoughts?" I asked, gently elbowing him.

By some mystery his smile grew, both in size and brightness. "This place is amazing!" He shouted, but then his face became slightly less joyous. He scooted closer to me and whispered this time. "Will you help me find a job?"

I let out a little chuckle as I talked.

"Oh, no, Stevvie you don't need to have a job." He looked at me with his eyebrows together and his eyes round, so I continued. "You're just a little kid, you aren't expected to work."

"Please, I really want one... please let me get a job." He sent his puppy-dog face my way when he begged.

"I mean... if you really want..."

"Oh, yes!" He jumped happily at the thought of being able to work for his stay.

"If you really want... I'll help you find something to do." I finished my sentence and smiled at his excited, silly-looking skipping about.

We stopped walking (and skipping) when Beck opened one of the classroom doors for us. "We'll be staying here for now. They have a lot of people to place, plus we shouldn't be here for too long."

"Why aren't we going to stay here long?" asked Stevvie.

"You can, but I'm heading back in a couple of days. The houses here are just a bit too permanent for my taste. I'm gonna grab some supplies, then head on home." He made a quick glance my way, as if asking if this would be the time I stay here.

I sighed.

"I'm going out to scavenge as soon as Stevvie's settled." The boy looked at me and seemed almost offended. Then a little smile showed on his face. A plan was very clearly brewing.

"I've picked a job... I'm going to scavenge."

"Good for you. Have fun finding a group," I said.

"You. If it's not too much trouble." The sneaky kid. I knew he could handle himself out there, with or without me, but I would rather he had someone to watch his back.

"No, it's no trouble at all." I guess this run to The Camp *was* mostly just to keep Beck company while he gathered supplies for the stops.

I dropped mine and Stevvie's bags by the door.

"Hey kid, come here, let's check that hand of yours." I pulled some medical supplies out of my backpack and waited for him.

He moved his hand from behind his back but kept it close to him. I shot him a quick look and stuck my palm out. Slowly, he caved. The bandage had become discolored from age and dirt, but also from a small amount of blood had leaked through.

I turned my body so he couldn't see. The injury had scabbed over, so I could see it better, but it had swollen as well.

"We should have De take a look at it to make sure it doesn't get infected, but it should be fine." I redressed the wound in clean gauze and patted his shoulder to signal to him 'all done'.

He smiled and ran to the door, grabbed his bag and dragged it to a cot in the corner. He pulled a worn-out deck of cards from the bag and settled onto the floor. Then started laying them out by number and color. He mumbled the numbers to himself as he placed them.

"Whatcha doing there kid?" Beck asked.

"Practicing," he said, fully focused on the cards in his hands and on the ground sprawled out in front of him.

"Practicing what?" He pried.

"Practicing my counting and my math." Beck let out an almost scoff-like breath at the kid's answer.

"Good. We need people who can count," he said after a moment, realizing that the kid was serious. Stevvie looked up at Beck and smiled widely with pride, then went back to the deck.

The lights were on now, but the sun was still out falling though, gradually falling beyond the horizon. I glanced between the two light sources, right on schedule as always.

The kid finished and packed the cards neatly back into his bag. He pulled off the oversized jacket and used it as a blanket.

Beck laid down on the floor and looked up to the lights. His arms rested under his head, and he closed his eyes and smiled. I followed his lead, drifting into a state of sleep.

The lights turned off, joined by the sound of electrical buzzing. I shot up, frighteningly familiar with the noise. The steady flow of dawn's light coming in from the window and several deep breaths calmed me down. I looked to the floor near the door to see Beck, who seemed to be trying to calm himself down as well, almost certainly scared awake from the lights like I had been.

I stood, grabbed my bag and headed to the locker rooms. It had been over a week since I'd taken an actual shower, but it felt much more like years.

Afterward, we all met up in front of the school just as we had planned. Time to introduce De. We lead the small group towards the back end of the camp, to De's house. I ran up to the door and knocked. It took a long time, but he did answer the door.

His stern thinking face was replaced by a wrinkled smile.

"Well... Well... Welcome back." He glanced over my shoulder before adding to his greeting. "Both of you."

"It's good to be back." Beck's voice was dull and false with a poorly hidden lie.

"Long term?" the doctor asked after a quick side hug.

"No, just temporary," I said as he hugged Beck.

"And who?" he pointed to the other three people among us.

"Stevvie, Daultin, Prince, and the little reason we're here." I introduced the three - no, four - of them.

De nodded his head and took a step back to invite us in. He did most of the talking as he explained how he could help in this situation. Despite his doctor jargon, the couple was soothed by his words.

They belonged here. They'd be able to grow here.

I left De's house early to try to get all of my preparation done. I planned to leave tomorrow, first thing, and in order to do so I needed to have my affairs in order. I grabbed my bag and headed to the river. I washed my laundry on a wash-board in a barrel, then hung them and walked to the farms. The Golden Garden in particular.

I gave the kid on duty some advice about rotations and water run-off from the green house. We called the large, glass box intended for farming 'The Golden Garden', because it gave us all food, even in the harshest of what winter had to throw at us. I also told the kid that Beck would need an order before the end of the week. Before returning to the school, I packed enough food for the rest of my travels.

At the school I grabbed some other things I thought I might need or want. Light books, paper, soap, some new clothes, and other things like that.

Heading back to our temporary room I bumped into Beck. His hair was slicked back, still wet from a shower. He ran his hands through it before speaking to me.

"I think De really rubbed off on them. The baby *should* be great." He smiled. I nodded my agreement and proceeded to tell him that I put in an order for his food and that he should grab some other supplies, sooner rather than later. He replied by lifting his obviously heavier bag.

We laid our bags down by the door and went into the cafeteria to eat. A breakfast of eggs and milk, they had bread, and Beck took a few slices but I didn't feel like having any of it.

After breakfast I went to see Bettsy. She was my favorite cow. I found her wandering the streets during one of my scavenging trips. Cut and tired, she didn't trust me, at least not at first. I had to lead her for over a week to make it back to The Camp, but it was well worth it.

Bettsy was as healthy and happy as ever, and she recognized me immediately and trotted up to greet me. Good news to end a visit with, always a plus.

I got an early start on the walking that needed to be done. Even without it I would make good time, as I walk faster alone. No people for me to protect or wait for.

Namma's House

    The silence was dull. It seemed like I was the only living thing for hundreds of miles. Everything was still and quiet, with only the sound of my breathing and the sand shifting beneath my weight.

    I came across the third stop, the house with the crazed; now dead - owner, but I didn't stay. I didn't even slow down, I only blankly watched the sun and kept moving.

    It was very risky to skip a stop, but I didn't want to stay there alone, so I took that risk. Someone died there only a few days ago, and the lights were probably damaged in the basement. There was too much horror movie spook happening there for me to stay. I would need to pick up the pace to make it to Namma's in time.

Small plants wilted in the heat. The rain could grow things, but they wouldn't survive the sun's unwavering fury for long. *I* could barely handle it. I pulled up my collar and had on some expired sunscreen, however the skin on my neck and face still reddened and split. One of my freckled cheeks burnt especially badly, it split and bled. The little trickle was hot, but colder still than its surroundings.

I shook my water jug, measuring how low it was. *I'll have to refill at Namma's.*

Light winds began to kick sand into the air, leaving behind the hard and cracked ground. The air-bound dust collected on my sweaty skin, turning into a thicker, muddy substance. *So much for that shower,* I thought, wiping the grimy paste off of my forehead. The light breeze shifted into a heavier gust. Even squinting and holding my hands in front of my face was pointless and painful, the sand still found its way into my eyes.

I nearly passed Namma's house, half blinded by the sand. It was late, but thankfully not yet dark, I had made the trip in a timely enough manner.

I knocked, wondering if she would hear me over the pelting of the windows and doors by the sand. And just like with the windows, my arms and face - where my skin was exposed - were being beaten and scratched by the ground as it was flung around by the wind.

The door swung open, but Namma caught it before the handle could put a hole in the wall. I walked in. It took all of the weight of her body to shut the door behind me, but she seemed to manage.

Still holding my bags, I stood in the hallway. There was a small awkwardness that built and filled the space.

She cleared her throat and showed her recognition of the weird quiet that hung in the room, breaking it with a smile. It wasn't often that we would be in the same room together without the company of Beck, so that was the source of the strange feeling.

Namma welcomed me further into the house with a wave of her arm, happy to see me.

Later, after the darkness covered the land and skies, I was digging through my bags for a rag to better wipe the sand from my skin. I found a box. At first, I had no recollection of its origin, but wanting to find out, I opened it. The small box was filled with round, blue treats. Beck's second specialty. I picked one up and let it roll along the indent of my palm. I popped it in my mouth. It's sweet, almost tart flavor filled my mouth and made it water. Unintentionally, I smiled and let out a low throaty laugh. I used the rag that I previously used to remove sand, to wipe some blueberry goo and drool off of my mouth.

Another extraordinary batch on Beck's part. It was a shame Stevvie didn't get to try some. He'll need to make more on a later date. At least the same quality of taste shouldn't be hard for him to do. That way, the boy would be able to enjoy it as well.

As I tried to close the box, a paper half taped to the lid folded over and got stuck in my way. The paper read 'If you get the time, I would love to hear the stories behind the boy. -Namma'.

I walked through the rooms looking for Namma and raised the paper when I located her.

"I can't. I don't really know a lot about him. He's a lot younger than he acts, and he's been through some crazy shit to get that way. But other than that, I don't know much. I try not to pry."

She glanced at the note in my hand to catch up with my end of the conversation before nodding her understanding.

"In that case... tell me about you. Anything new?"

I knew what she was asking about, or more so *who*, but decided it better to pretend like I didn't.

"Nope. I think we're almost past the hot days, but nothing more than that."

"The weather. That's *all*?"

She attempted a deeper dig.

"I got to see Betsy. Miss that old girl sometimes." She sighed and rolled her eyes lightly. She flattened her dress as she walked out of the room, leaving me standing around dusty furniture and old cots, all alone in the full, yet empty, room.

I left the room, and as I did I could have sworn that I saw the lights flicker. The room spun and made me dizzy, I leaned against the door frame, frozen with fear. The spinning slowed while I convinced myself that it was nothing more than my eyesight. *I'm safe, I'm in the light,* I thought, to reassure myself.

After taking several deep breaths, the room stilled again, and I pulled myself off of the door frame, I shook my head, and finished leaving that room.

I woke up the next morning, and after getting ready to leave I said goodbye to Namma. She was somehow already sitting at the table, sipping a hot drink from a mug. She nodded a 'goodbye', with a wave of her hand. I grabbed my bags, and I left. To the porch, where I sat until the sun finished rising, which took less time than I expected it would.

I was surprised that I could miss the wind, but I could and did, for without it the sun felt even hotter. At one point I held my bag over my head in a feeble attempt to hide from the sun.

I walked like that until my arms hurt and I gave into the fact that I would just be burnt.

I tried to open the door of Beck's house, but it was locked, which seemed a little out of character for him, but also smart. I got the 'key' from Beck's hiding spot in a hole under a rock. It was not a duplicate, as it was very hard to find someone who could make keys these days, but Beck had bent some metal that worked well enough.

Inside the house was almost the same temperature as it was outside, but at least the sun would stop trying to burn off all of the best of my skin.

I took a deep breath, letting the smell of this house fill my body. I held it there, saving the first breath after opening the door for as long as I could. I let it go in a relaxed sigh. Smiling, I closed the door behind me.

The slightly colder and shadowed air on my skin was refreshing, but some cool water would be almost infinitely better. I made my way to the bathroom, stopping on my way to turn on the house's lights. The water ran brown for a second, making me gag, and I had to hold back throw up. It was not something I expected, and it disgusted me. The color lightened, but still didn't run clear. I wiped the nothing from my hands to my pants as I made my way to the basement, extra careful to stay under the light. I grabbed a box of tools and began a clumsy attempt to fix the water pump.

I heard the sound of a car's tires pulling up the dirt as it drove up to the house. The sound genuinely scared me, as I hadn't heard a car in a long while. I ran a rag between my hands to clean them and crept quickly to the front door.

Beck walked through it, barely registering the change in light before he spoke.

"Hey, Namma said you left. We need you to come with us." He started to walk back through the door. "Prince is in labor, and she wants you to be there, she wants a familiar face around."

"What?" I said, wanting a little more information. To catch up with him, I ran out of the door.

"She doesn't know many people, especially not a lot of women and she wanted you to be there. Honestly, so do I," he said, jumping into the car after me.

We don't use cars often, as gasoline was hard to come by, but for certain time-sensitive emergencies, we made an exception.

"What are we waiting for? Let's go." I said, hitting the outside of the door with my hand and leaving it hanging out of the open window. The person in the driver's seat hit the gas and the vehicle lurched forward, we were off to deliver a baby.

Pillars of dust rose up behind us as we drove. Every small movement pushed us around on the seats. Most of the seatbelts were broken so there wasn't anything to keep us in place. I was both awkwardly put on the spot and touched by the fact that Prince wanted me there, enough to convince someone to borrow a car.

In what seemed like no time at all we had passed all of the stops, which had taken me days to walk. The speed kept moving the wind around me and made my hair stab me in the eyes. I pulled it into a messy ponytail to combat it.

We drove up to The Camp. The person in the driver's seat waved to the guards at the gate, and they slowed for a second before going in. We turned to the right and stopped at the school.

I ran into the school and followed Beck through its halls. We knew we were getting closer the louder Prince's screams got. We stopped just in front of the doors when the screaming stopped. We knocked with caution, and a moment later, De opened it, letting us in.

Prince was holding her baby, exhausted and glossy with sweat, but with a huge smile on her face. De was wrapping Daultin's hand, but he didn't seem to notice as all of his attention was on the tiny, sleepy child wrapped cozily in his wife's arms.

I stood in the doorway with Beck, neither of us knowing quite what to do. The room stayed the same while several minutes passed by. Daultin looked up, noticed us and waved for us to come meet the baby. We were nervous and cautious but moved toward them nonetheless.

We walked up to them slowly, trying not to wake the baby. He had his little hand wrapped around Prince's index finger. He was so peaceful, swaddled in that blanket and fast asleep, with what looked like a smile on his face.

Beck draped his arm over my shoulder and pulled me into a side hug, smiling down at the little infant. Even De let himself smile when he saw the baby.

"I'm late for this thing... if you need anything else just have one of these two come get me." He poked a finger at Beck and myself. "There are a stack of baby - and parenting - books on the shelf over there. Take them, read up, it'll help out with some of the questions that you might have." They said their goodbyes and he left.

We stayed a little while longer, but not horribly long because we wanted them to get some rest. When we were in the hallway, Beck's walking slowed to a stop. I turned to see him tearing up. I pulled him into a hug holding back tears of my own. The swirl of both joy and mourning between us pulled the tears to the surface. We stayed there crumpled under the weight of our shared sorrow, even if my throat could speak over the lump that grew in it, I wouldn't have the words to help him or myself.

He took a step back, smiled at me and linked our arms at their elbows. He started walking, dragging me with him. A calmness settled across his face.

"That baby was *adorable*." I squealed.

"And so fucking tiny!" he joined in, adding to my squealing. We hadn't seen more than maybe one or two babies since the beginning of the Finish. It had become a strange sight, they were only little, dumb people, and yet it had become taboo.

I went to get ready for bed and realized I'd left my bag at Beck's house near the front door but I chose to do nothing about it. Tired from the day's travels, both on foot and in a hot car, I laid down and slept. Poor Prince. The whole lot of them must be so tired that they could sleep for days.

When I woke, Beck and Stevvie were still out cold. A light snore came from one of them, but I couldn't figure out its exact owner. My thoughts swung back to my backpack, and how Stevvie could try one of the treats still tucked away in the box. Hopefully they would still be as good.

I sat there under a blanket and waited for them to wake up. I got bored in almost no time, started fidgeting, and cleaned underneath my fingernails. By the time they rose, I was tapping out musical rhythms on my thighs and humming along to them, which was probably what woke them.

Beck looked at me, yawned and started to lay down to go back to sleep.

"No, don't go back to sleep, I'm so bored!" I whispered. He waved his hand at me and rolled over to face the wall. I scoffed, and he replied by letting out a silent torso-shaking chuckle. He turned to face me, stood up, and walked to where I was in the room.

"Yay, he's awake!"

He waved his hand at me once again and made a sharp turn to leave the room. I caught him trying to hide a smile as he left, and he didn't bother to close the door behind him.

Stevvie sat up and stretched. He opened his eyes one at a time, struggling to keep them from closing again. He opened and closed his mouth a few times, it made clicking sounds. The kid stood up and walked past me, into the hall. I was sure that he knew as little about where he was going as I did.

The room felt bigger now that I was alone, but it was still very small, with all of the desks stacked against the far wall.

I leaned out of the doorway, into the also empty hall. I walked to the middle of the room again and spun in pointless circles. After checking my surroundings, I started to dance simply because my body felt a need to move. It wasn't graceful and there wasn't music to follow, but I felt like dancing, and it felt good.

I heard someone walking a while later and it startled me into stopping. They continued past, not knowing I was in here. I saw them through the window but didn't know them. That put a smile on my face, the mystery of strangers could exist even in such a small community at the end of humanity.

I went back to the bed, not able to pick anything else to pass the time until well after the sun came up. I sat there and waited for either of the boys to come back. I knew I would have some work to do around The Camp, but for now I did nothing.

Beck stood over me. I hadn't noticed that I had fallen back to sleep. My surprise made him turn and spit up the water he was drinking. He coughed out a laugh and caught his breath before shaking his head and taking another gulp.

"The kid is waiting for you in the lunchroom. He sent me to come get you." I got up and walked out with him, avoiding the puddle of slobber-water as we left.

I only realized that I was hungry when the smells of food hit me. My stomach growled in anticipation, loud enough that Beck looked at me.

"What? I'm hungry." I said, defensively covering my rumbling stomach.

We went to the end of the line to get some food and both started looking around for Stevvie.

The little kid had already scarfed down most of what was laying on his plate by the time we found him. The entire cafeteria was buzzing with chatter about the baby. The Camp had had some pregnancies, but it was difficult for any to end on such a good note as this one had.

Stevvie looked to us as we sat down and wiggled in his chair placing his hands on the table to keep from falling over. A group of people walked by talking loudly about the new baby boy, and Stevvie gave us a look.

"Still want to meet the kid?" I asked. He nodded so much that he lost his balance a little, grabbing the edge of the table harder to stabilize himself. He still wobbled.

He watched intensely as we ate our food. I could see that Beck was eating exceptionally slowly to try to get to him, so I joined. The kid didn't seem to notice. He did, however, see that we were chuckling at something, and he looked confused. A good long minute passed. People walked in and out before we even got close to leaving. The moment Beck set his fork down, Stevvie was on his feet.

Stevvie looked at the baby with such a strange, but happy expression, it was clear he hadn't seen a baby before. Prince and Daultin were sharing a house with three other people who were all making the same face as Stevvie. Prince leaned forward to hand the baby to her husband.

"I have to pee. I'll be back in a minute." She stood up shakily and walked out of the room.

Daultin shrugged a shoulder lightly after her, his attention went back to cradling the baby and rocking from side to side.

"Alright, we should probably get going now. It'll be too late soon." I tapped Stevvie on the shoulder as I spoke, and we said our goodbyes. Before leaving the front gate, and after getting the boys' luggage, we ran into De.

He gave us a nod and a wrinkly almost-smile. Looking over his shoulder, the smile went away and he nodded up to the people on the wall. Without turning back to look at us, he shifted on his heels and left.

We walked through the vastly open gate into the world. We had a long way to go, and with much less time than I would like, we set off.

It was kind of nice to walk with other people, less quiet. Even when the conversations drifted off there was the sound of footsteps. The boys talked about how they each learned math. Stevvie couldn't remember exactly how he had learned, he just knew it and used the cards to practice and remember. Beck learned like most people of the past, in school. Beck told Stevvie how boring school was, but the kid seemed in a trance at the thought of it all.

I stayed quiet, listening to the six feet pounding against the ground and the words the other two shared. I zoned out listening to Stevvie pepper Beck with questions and Beck responding.

Eventually the chat of school stopped, because we reached the third stop and because Beck seemed a bit annoyed.

The house without lights. The house where Beck had killed a crazed man just days ago.

We walked in from the front, where we - without speaking a word - decided we'd stay. You could see the back of the house untouched by anyone as it sat in darkness. You could see the blood stained floor, blackened and warped from the thick liquid. And if you leaned, maybe squinted, you could see a circle of wax puddles that were once candles but were now burnt onto the floor.

I closed my eyes and could almost feel it all. The stench of blood and lingering smoke, the crying woman wailing in another language, all of it. The smells and sounds were replaced by the faded stench of dirt and sweat that we had brought in with us. I opened my eyes.

Tired from walking, we drank water, set up lights, opened some canned food, and were asleep barely before the sun went down.

I slept deeply. Some time in the night I felt a small shift in gravity, and it was enough to wake me. A spare shirt was draped over my eyes. Still, the light leaked through the fabric to meet me. My limbs were tired, stiff, and I felt like I was being held in place. I shouted and jumped up, almost out of my skin. I fell hard on my butt, the cloth fell off of my eyes to let me see Beck standing above me. His arms were hanging out in front of him as if he was carrying something invisible.

He was confused and holding back the urge to laugh at my pointless little stir of panic. I gathered my limbs beneath me and stood, dizzy from so suddenly waking up. We were back in the vast open desert, Beck stood above me with a hand over his mouth.

"Why're you freakin' out?" he asked through a hum like chuckle.

"How did I fall?" I ignored his question and asked my own.

"I tried to wake you up, but you were *not* having it. So, I carried you. You were out cold until just a second ago." I vaguely remembered telling someone to let me sleep in, realizing now that it wasn't a part of a dream.

"Thanks? I can take it from here though."

He nodded and we jogged a few steps forward to where Stevvie had stopped to wait for us.

Next on the list was Namma's house.

Scavenging

We had many conversations about where the kid was going to stay, even though he couldn't pick where he wanted to be. It seemed like we wouldn't find any answer at all, until Stevvie reminded me that he wanted to go scavenging. He was so excited to be out in the world, and for once not be alone while he explored, I just see it.

Stevvie and I decided to go on a scavenger's run. Whenever we got back then we would find a more permanent home for him. Hesitant to leave Beck, I came up with excuses to wait at his house for a few extra days. Eventually, he caught on and convinced me to go by saying,

"Next time you're around here, I'll open the door welcomingly - no gun this time." He smiled, and it made me smile back.

I started to walk away, but I paused when I realized I had forgotten something. I turned, reached in my bag and handed Beck a small jar of blueberry jam. He looked at the jar, then to me. He nodded and waited for me to leave. I turned, taking a last glance at him still standing there. He half raised his hand in a wave and I did the same, then I looked to Stevvie and left.

The kid and I spent the first few days walking and the first few nights sitting under flashlights hung from trees or poles or anything tall enough to keep us safe. The buildings, mostly rubble now, got closer together the longer we walked. That is when we started to duck into the buildings, pulling apart drawers and shuffling through cabinets. We grabbed bags and filled them with anything of any use.

"When you're scavenging, think kind of like a hoarder. Do you know what that is?" He shook his head. I sighed, trying to think of how to explain the concept to him. "If it has a use, or even if you think it might eventually be of use, keep it." I lifted up a medication bottle. "Like this... I have no clue what it is or what it does, but it might be the one thing De needs the most right now."

I tucked it into one of my backpacks. He looked lost in thought for a minute but quickly snapped out of it, nodded, and got to work. He picked up another bottle of pills, shook it to tell how much was still in it, and stuffed it into his bag. Without turning to look at me, he left, hesitating momentarily to grab an unstained rag from the wall. This room was done, this apartment was done, onto the next one.

This continued on for days, until we were carrying so much that we debated traveling further in multiple trips. Instead we decided to go back, trying our best not to continue scavenging the buildings as we walked through our return.

At last we made it back to Beck's house. We dropped all of the scavenged supplies on the front lawn, feeling too dead now to carry them further. We walked through the front door. Beck paused his walking for a moment and spun in a circle. When he got dizzy and stopped spinning, he was smiling.

"No gun. I told you so," he said, continuing to walk toward us. I smiled and shook my head. "What are you doing on my property?" he said in a tone, mocking himself.

I stuck out my hand for him to shake, he grabbed it and pulled me into a hug.

"A long time to be off scavenging, but it seems to have paid off. That's one heck of a haul," he said, looking out the still open door at the stack of bags as he slid out of our hug.

He helped us drag the new supplies into the house after welcoming Stevvie back with a kindly 'hello'.

It was dark outside now as we all sat around the table. It was quiet. I glanced up from my food to see Beck deep in thought, examining his fork. It wasn't even a particularly interesting fork, but it had his full and undivided attention.

"A test." He spoke as if we had heard his entire train of thought. He saw the confusion on our faces and explained his sudden burst of volume. "We can't decide where the kid should stay..." He waited emptily for us to catch on. "So let's do a test, to decide for us." He looked at Stevvie, who nodded what I assumed was his agreement.

"You pick the test, Stevvie, and the 'prize' house, like a heads or tails."

"Guns, tomorrow. Here." He stood up, trying to hold back a smile. He nodded once and walked away, and Beck and I shared the same surprised expression at his exit.

"Guns it is, I guess," I said. "But do you *really* think you could beat him?" I was mocking, and Beck responded to it by shrugging.

Both of us thought about it seriously for a second as our brains leaped to the desert with the snake incident. The question lost its mocking tone as it hung in the air. *Could he beat him? Did he* want *Stevvie to lose?*

It would probably be better if the kid went back to the camp and joined a more stable family. But what then? If he were to be too grownup for that - too much of an adult to get along with other young children? He may be young, but his life - has been spent in nothing but the wild of the Finish.

I grabbed my bag, glad to be reunited with my few belongings, and headed to the basement to take a cold shower. Afterward, I laid down in the bay window. My cold, wet hair pressed against the frame of glass, a cool breeze leaked in through the cracks it had and I fell asleep.

This time, again, I was the first one up. I ran to turn off the lights, because the sun was high and bright and they weren't of any use like this. The loud click woke up Stevvie who went to wake Beck. Then the two stood tiredly staring at me, matching with their brown bed-head hair do's. We had all slept in.

We moved the gathering to the yard. A good distance from a line of cans, the boys were setting up to play with their guns.

"Care if I shoot first?" Beck asked. Stevvie took a step back, as a non-verbal 'go ahead.' Beck lined his gun up an arm's length in front of his face, a large, gray, more modern pistol, and he fired.

The bang of the bullet leaving its casing joined almost instantly by a soft pinging sound as the bullet ripped through a can and pulled it out of its place.

He smiled and looked at the kid. Stevvie took the bait and stepped forward to get closer to the task. He lifted his revolver to the sight of the cans still standing and shot off three bullets in astonishingly little time. None of the cans had budged, they stood perfectly unscathed.

Beck smiled, not at the boy losing, but instead at the boy's losing an unwinnable bet. He smiled at the inevitable, made a clicking noise and shrugged.

"Guess you aren't as good as I thought."

Stevvie stuck one of his little fingers in the air to silence Beck, then turned the finger to the cans. He sighed after a moment of our confusion and waved for us to follow as he walked away.

He stopped at the line of cans and pointed to a stump one of them was resting on. He leaned close and tapped the grooved wood. Three tiny holes, so close together that you could have easily thought that they were one. The holes steamed some from the heat of the bullets against the deadened wooden grain.

Beck's face lifted with astonishment and his shoulders fell from defeat.

"Welcome to your new-ish home, kid," he said, turning to wave his hands at the house.

Stevvie perked up. "So, I can stay?"

"It was a deal," Beck responded, looking back to the tree stump with an intrigued, respectful smile.

... Almost Three Years Ago ...

She stood with a level of confidence that shadowed even Beck's. I, however, was doubtful of that confidence.

No one had beaten Beck in the battle of bullets, of course there is a first for everything. He had already made an amazing shot ripping a can from its place and throwing it into an ocean of air, so this was most likely not going to be that 'first time for everything' kind of situation. Still, she showed no fear of failure as she aimed and fired twice. One was close, but neither made it where she had intended them to.

She ran and hugged him.

"Thanks, for not taking it easy on me, old man."

"Hey, you know I wouldn't." He hollered after her as she ran back to practice aiming without shooting. He looked at me, smiled and rolled his eyes, her confidence not wavered by the failure.

... Present ...

Beck glanced at the kid as we were walking back into the house. A memory crossed his mind, a once forgotten memory it seemed, by the way he smiled. The little kid started singing some nonsense to himself, joyed by the outcome of the day. Beck heard the kid's singing, and he was pulled from his thoughts. He rolled his eyes and smiled at me.

Something of the day felt familiar. I couldn't quite place my finger on it, something like a memory now long forgotten hung from the tip of my tongue and left a strange taste.

I returned a smile to Beck.

"So, what are we going to do for the rest of the day?" I asked Stevvie. He shrugged and wandered off, still singing incoherently at the top of his lungs.

The day was more than half over, but I did have the perfect idea for an activity. I ran and grabbed my bag, calling to the boys as I dug through it. A 'huzzah' slipped my lips as I found what I was looking for.

"They're better when they're fresh, but still not bad," I said, opening the small box and sitting on the floor now that we were inside.

The boys followed my lead and sat down with me. Beck was analyzing every bit of Stevvie's reaction. Though he had seen it on every other person who had tried those blueberry treats, he was still anticipating that which would come. The box was empty in no time at all. Stevvie absolutely loved them. He enjoyed having dessert for the first time - homemade, at least.

Stevvie looked at his hand. Carefully, he peeked under the bandage.

"How's it looking?" Beck asked.

The boy shrugged.

"Doesn't hurt too much anymore, but it looks kinda gross." The way he said it added a humored edge, and Beck and I lightly chuckled.

We spent the rest of what daylight lingered in the sky moving around furniture and setting up the guest room to be officially for Stevvie. I thought he had gotten excited to have a *bed* for himself - but an entire room... he nearly burst to bits from the excitement.

Beck stood in the doorway looking in on us. He ran his hand down the notches, the paint covered them, but not a hundred percent, it was clear he could still feel the grooves beneath the layers. His eyes closed with pain as he traced the paint.

... Almost Two Years Ago ...

I walked into the house, the thick, intoxicating smell of paint filled my lungs and choked out the oxygen. I swung the front door open and closed again and again, coughing and trying to air out the house.

I covered my face with a fistful of my shirt and went to find Beck. He was standing limply in the doorway of the now vacant room, drenched in paint and crying to himself. I grabbed his arm and ripped the paintbrush from his grasp. He barely seemed able to stand, like his spine was the only thing keeping him from falling.

I realized what he was painting, and I went absolutely berserk, screaming and flailing my arms about the air at him, paint flung through the air and rained down on us just as my angered words did.

He dropped to his knees and fell onto the wall. I couldn't hear what I had screamed at him, but I could feel it heavy in my chest. I just stood there, shocked and suddenly silent.

When he spoke, his voice was quiet and shaky.

"I can't do it," he said. "I can't keep looking at all of the..." His voice broke. "Little reminders, but I... can't just get rid of her, either." He looked at his hands. The paint that coated them was white, but I knew that through his eyes... all he saw was red.

I hadn't realized it right away, but I had fallen to the ground in front of him. I knew what he meant. She wasn't just in small things around the house, she was also in his head, having been left there by his heart.

I grabbed his face in my hands and lifted it. The circles under his eyes were so dark that they looked like bruises, and I could have bet money I had a matching set. I pulled his head to my shoulder, resting my face on his and told him, "I know." Although it was only two words, such a simple statement, it was all that was needed to be said.

... Present ...

He took a deep breath and said goodnight to Stevvie before he left the doorway to go turn on the lights.

I followed him, because he had waved for me to do so. He asked a question to break the silence.

"Are you moving back here, now that the kid has?"

I stopped moving.

He noticed this and turned to me.

"I don't know, am I?"

"If you want to, you're more than welcome."

I smiled.

"Okay then, I guess I am."

He turned, but I could tell he was smiling too, and he flipped on the lights. He walked away, leaving me alone. *Did I just move in? Just like that?* I thought to myself. *I think I did.*

I slept in the makeshift bedroom in the basement, leaving my things piled in one corner.

When I woke up it was still dark outside. I didn't want to wake the boys, so I decided to read an old law book I had. The time slipped away as the pages turned, and within the words I lost track of time.

Beck came skipping down the basement stairs and over to the empty doorway to the room I was in.

"Breakfast."

I tucked a folded piece of paper in between the pages of the book to save my place before trotting to catch up with him.

Breakfast was simple. It was the gruel-like substance which was often served at The Camp. This particular batch tasted especially gross.

"You may make great candy," I gagged a little after swallowing. "But this is disgusting," I said to Beck, gesturing to the bowl of mush in front of me.

"Oh really? So, what do you think, Stevvie?" He turned from me to address the boy.

Stevvie choked down a mouthful and shivered dramatically. I copied his lead, to which Beck rolled his eyes at us and pulled out a bag of sugar from a nearby cupboard.

"You don't know what you're talking about," he said, stuffing a spoonful of the goop into his mouth, gagging, and spitting it back into the bowl. "Pass the sugar," he said in defeat, disgusted and not wanting to take another bite of the *uniquely* flavored food.

Stevvie and I stifled our laughter as best we could as we powdered sugar into our food.

The kid went outside to play in the fresh air after breakfast. Some clouds had rolled in and it wasn't too hot anymore. I decided to do the dishes, they had been piling up and they had begun to smell so they desperately needed to be done. I cracked a window and filled the sink, poured a small amount of liquid dish soap in half of it, and got to cleaning. I rinsed and scrubbed the food off of the dishes in the other half.

When I was about half finished, Beck came to my side. He dried the dishes I had already washed and put them away. He was humming something and almost dancing around the kitchen.

"What song is that?" I asked after the melody changed for what seemed to be the fourth time.

"Huh?" He looked at me with a tilted head and crinkled eyebrows, a plate hanging loosely in his hand.

"The song you were just humming, what is it called?" I clarified.

I saw as the gears in his head clicked into place.

"I don't know. I can't remember. I'm not even sure that I remember how it goes." He must have thought that that was more than enough of an explanation, so he went back to drying the dishes and humming the mystery song.

After a while we were just playing with the fading suds in the sink. Acting like children, as we messed with the dirty dish water. I was so glad to see Beck as himself, or the version of him that I used to know, even if it was just for a moment.

Beck lifted a handful of the little bubbles to his face.

"Oh, how did my beard get so long and gray so fast?" he joked, stroking the suds stuck to his chin. "And why are they so white? I'm not old enough to have white hair yet!"

"Are you so sure about that?" I pointed to his head and squinted, jumping at his offended expression.

"Oh... What did you just say to me?" he asked, using his real voice now. I tried to run from him, but he caught me quickly and pulled me into a hug. "No come on, tell me what you said," he commanded as he tickled my sides.

I squirmed out of his arms.

"You're old!" I shouted, still joking around with him, and I took off running.

"I'm *barely* older than you." He hollered after me as we ran out the front door.

We ran circles around Stevvie until all three of us were dizzy.

"You *are* old," Stevvie agreed with me.

Beck waved his hand in response, not having enough air to spout out a comeback fitting for the taunt. He looked up at the cloudy sky, trying to measure how much of the day had already gone by.

I realized that soon clouds, almost exactly like the ones overhead now, would bring with them snow and much shorter days. That of course brought on the worry about crops, warmth and light.

Daylight meant energy and safety. With less light, *would* there be enough energy to create and keep safety during the longer, darker hours? Would we have to stay at The Camp throughout the cold days? And with such large numbers, would The Camp even be a safe place for us?

I shook the thought from my head and focused instead on the thick, warm air all around me. Though it wasn't *as* warm as it had been, we were still in the warm days. The heat pushed the worry out of my head for the current moment.

We were all lying on the ground looking at the sky now. I leaned over and wiped the few remaining bubbles out of Beck's stubble. He didn't look at me, but he smiled.

Beck rolled over onto his stomach and pulled his favorite knife out of his pocket. He pulled a weed out of the ground, rolled onto his back, flipped open the blade, and started sliding it through the plant. He held it upside-down and pressed the knife into the branching off points of its stems. After it was shed of its limbs, he lifted it to the sky, pleased with his work.

He let his hand drop to his stomach and sat up. Without realizing it, I followed his actions. He leaned forward, looking at the plant in his hand, deep in thought. He glanced up to see Stevvie sleeping, before he decided to speak.

"What happened?"

"To?"

"Us."

"Oh... I don't know." It was close enough to the truth, I didn't know *all* of what had happened to us.

He sighed and rolled his eyes, not fully believing my answer either.

"I do." He paused, not sure if what he was going to say next would be too much of a conversation, one we wouldn't be able to handle. "And I'm sorry." I tried to speak but he beat me to it. "I know you had to deal with it yourself and I shouldn't have made you deal with me too. It was wrong, and I just wanted to finally apologize to you."

I reached over and grabbed his hand. This shocked him, but it got his attention, nonetheless. I gave his hand a mild and reassuring squeeze, showing my forgiveness. He smiled at that.

"Things may never be the way they were before, but I'm glad, in a way. 'Cause things are the way they are now, different, difficult, with way too much history, and that is how it is."

He nodded his understanding and agreement.

He picked his knife from off of the ground where he had dropped it, closed it and shifted his weight to put it back in his pocket. He took one last glance at the dismembered weed before he flicked it off to the side. Beck carried Stevvie into the house, and I walked with them. Beck let the kid sleep.

I decided to make lunch and just store the kid's food until he woke up. I handed Beck some food and sat at the table after having cleaned up. It was simple sandwiches, but still much better than that morning's breakfast. He sat across from me.

"So, I was thinking, when are you going to set up a farm here?"

"If you want one, and if the land agrees with that desire, then any time I can get someone to help me." He took a bite after responding.

"Really?" He nodded. "So, plant before the cold days, so we can have solid crops next year?"

"Now?" he asked.

"If I can get someone to help me." He halfway smiled at me when I attempted to speak in a lower voice like his.

"We'll mark the ground and put up a fence and get started tomorrow. Then when that's done, we can go to The Camp and get the supplies." He said, making a plan so that this could actually happen.

"Sounds good. It's a plan. We'll rip up the ground and plant the seeds. What are we gonna grow?" I asked. It was his land; it was his choice.

"We can all discuss it in the morning. Before we start putting up a fence, we'll need to know how much room we're gonna need." Apparently, this was all *our* land now - the three of us - and it had been a long time since things had been that way.

What was left of the rest of the day rushed by pretty quickly, even through the anticipation of the work we would do to build the farm. Once all of the crops - currently undecided - grew fully, how often would we go to The Camp? How often would we *need* to?

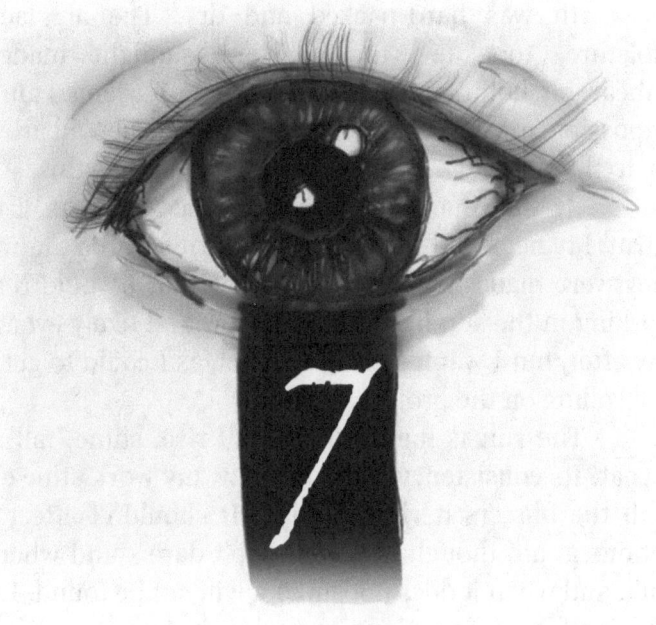

Farming

    It was early. The sun had only been up for a few minutes, but sweat already pulled itself into beads on my skin. The air was still and quiet, all except for the sounds of the shovels tearing apart the ground. We had decided to grow a larger field of wheat and corn - perhaps other things like that - and a small garden-like area for fruits and vegetables.

    We had measured how much land we wanted to use to grow - the patch that seemed the least deadened - and were now digging to put small wooden poles in place. After the poles were secure, we would wrap barbed wire between them, stopping not much higher than our knees.

Today there were no longer clouds above; they had moved on. Not leaving behind any sign of their existence, the earth was hard-packed and dry. The air lacked moisture, too, and the constant sunlight made it unbearably hot, making it all the worse. It seemed almost impossible for the cold days to ever come when all around us, to the very edge of the sky, was weather like this.

By the time the sun had reached its peak, I was burnt. My neck and the backs of my arms weren't tanned: they were made raw and red. I knew that I would regret working in the sun like this tomorrow and likely even the day after, but I wanted to do as much as I could to get the ball rolling on the project at hand.

The sun is inevitable: it will rise, shine, fall and repeat. Its consistency shouldn't slow my work ethic even with the blisters it risks leaving. It shouldn't affect my actions at all, though it does. I don't dare stand where it isn't, and when it does not shine, I will not be found. Even now it affected my actions, by making me want to quit.

We continued the routine of Beck and me digging, switching off who holds the poles for the other as they pour and pack the dirt back into the holes. All the while, Stevvie sat on the porch and watched us. He begged for us to let him help and though his mind was grown, his body was not. He could barely carry the shovel when it was empty, and the poles were entirely out of the question, especially with the cut still trying to heal on his right hand.

But he didn't give in so easily. He wanted something to do, to feel useful. So, we had him bring water, to make sure that no matter how hard we work, the three of us would not get dehydrated. He didn't like the job, but he took it, because at the very least it was better than doing nothing.

We had been running at full steam, but we had almost nothing to show for it. When the dark started to sneak up on us (we caught it in time, but it was still a surprise) there were only a few sturdy poles in the ground. This was going to take longer than I thought.

I took a quick shower. Even the cold water burned my skin where it had been exposed to the sun. I dug through my bag, but I couldn't find any clean shirts, not even semi-clean shirts. I did, however, find a pair of shorts and some underwear. I looked through the drawers in the basement room, where I got lucky and found one of Beck's old button-ups.

I went to bed without going upstairs again.

I woke up very early, probably just a few short hours after falling asleep. I had a nightmare about *her*, but I couldn't remember the specifics after sleep left me. I rubbed my arm across my eyes and straightened my back in a stretch. I stood and made my way out of the basement. I got a drink of water and wandered back to bed. I couldn't sleep again. I tried for what felt like hours to be able to sleep, but I simply couldn't.

Beck squirmed, but he didn't wake. I tapped his shoulder again, same results. I rolled my eyes and lightly shoved his arm. He mumbled something tiredly, and for all I knew he wasn't even speaking English. The room was quiet for a moment, and I felt awkward just standing over him, watching. He broke the silence.

"What?" His voice was clearer now, but still groggy.

"What 'what'?" I asked.

I could feel his eyes roll. He sighed and shifted his face away from the lights and into the pillow. "What do you want? It's the middle of the night; what *could* you possibly want?"

"How do you know it's night?" I asked, ignoring his questions.

Another eye roll.

"Answer me."

"I can't sleep."

"I wonder what that's like," he said, with sarcasm sharply aimed at me for not allowing him to go back to sleep. A short pause, then a sigh from me got him talking again. "What do you want *me* to do about that?"

"Stay awake with me."

"No." His voice was stern and unwilling to waver.

"Pleas-"

"No." He cut me off at the beginning of my long bout of begging and pulled the blanket over the back of his head. "Just go to sleep."

"Can't."

"Try."

"I did."

"Try again." He growled.

I paused before talking and he got so quiet that I thought he had fallen back to sleep.

"It's *her*. I had a nightmare."

Without making a noise, without ignoring me or even trying to tell me to go back to sleep, he got up. His eyes weren't open as he stumbled his way to the closet. He slid on a flannel shirt and rubbed his eyes to fight the sleep.

He walked to the doorway, turned to me and spoke.

"You make me get up, but then you don't even come with me?" He waved for me to follow him. I smiled and jogged to close the few steps between us.

Beck froze as I walked past him. He grabbed my arm and spun me around to face him. "This shirt?"

"I found it. I ran out of clothes. I'll wash it and get it back to you." I rambled on, hoping he wouldn't get mad.

A crooked smile broke across his face. "I've been looking for this shirt. It's one of my favorites." He set his hand on my shoulder and with a finger traced the pattern.

"I'll give it back to you." I repeated. "Promise."

He leaned closer, letting go of my arm to set that same hand against the side of my face. His smile deepened and he stared into my eyes.

"Keep it." He backed up and walked past me, buttoning up his shirt as the cold air kicked in. I turned and walked after him. *What was that?*

We talked each other's ears off until Stevvie woke up and walked into us sitting at the table laughing. He smiled, waved to us, and turned off the lights. I hadn't realized the sun was up to join our liveliness.

Beck offered to make the disgusting goop, but none of us wanted that. None of us were even hungry at the time. Instead of eating, we decided to get an early jump on the work.

My legs were burning quicker than my arms today in shorts. But my arms still hurt and had just begun to peel. Beck realized this and stood so I would be in his shadow. It took me a moment to notice, but once I did, it was obvious.

I was glad today was another sunny day, and it was all the better now that the sun couldn't reach me as well. His shirt was too large, and I kept having to push the sleeves up. I tried rolling them instead, and it worked well enough.

After a while we did begin to feel hungry and went to eat. Afterwards, we worked again towards putting up the fence. This routine of eat sleep and work repeated for several days. It went on until eventually the fence was finished. Stevvie had to be lifted over it. When it was done, the barbed wire went too high up for him to jump over.

"We should get seeds before breaking apart the ground. Which means a trip to The Camp," I said, and the boys nodded in agreement. We were lucky that Beck had enough supplies for the fence. "When should we leave?"

"As soon as possible. Gotta get it over with before the cold comes."

"Tomorrow?" Stevvie suggested.

"Sounds good to me." I joined in on the conversation.

Like we had planned, the next day we began walking to The Camp. Thankfully, the last few days of our journey were cloudy. It had even been raining. All of our clothes were like weights with the rain, and the ground wanted to hold onto our shoes in between each of our steps.

We only spent one night at The Camp. We grabbed the supplies we had come for and went to sleep. We said hello, then goodbye, and left to get back to build the rest of the farm.

A few days later, we walked back onto Beck's property, our property, and refreshed our memories of where exactly each crop would go. We dug up the ground, all three of us. We did it in rows, ripped up the soil and sprinkled it with seeds. This took almost no time at all compared to fencing off the area. The farm was finally completed.

Maybe, eventually, we hoped to add some animals to the land, though if we didn't, it would only keep us an excuse to have to go back to The Camp.

We finished just in time for the first wave of frost, not two whole days after finishing, the earth was covered in a thin, hard layer of ice. By afternoon the ground was back to its natural color, but it was still solid as rock.

It was getting dark outside. The lights were already on in the house, but I couldn't seem to get myself off of the porch. I couldn't stop staring in wonder at the work that had been done and the fact that - come the next long string of warm days - that barren, fenced off chunk of land would be lush with growing things.

I was pulled out of my state of wonder-stricken thinking by a rustle near the end of the porch, the bit farthest from where I sat. I paused, waiting to see whether I had imagined it or if it was just the wind. A slight chill hung in the motionless, windless air.

It happened again, a soft rustling, this time followed by another sound - almost a cry.

I got up, wiped some dust from my hands onto my pants, and I went to investigate. I leaned over the edge of the porch, holding onto the railing for support. Lying there in the few plants that still dared to stand, was a puppy. 'Dog', or 'mut', would have suited it better than the title of 'puppy', it was dirty and covered in blood, cowering and growling at the very sight of me. Its hair stood on end, and it jumped backwards, not having the footing to run.

I jumped off of the porch after assessing the situation. It seemed harmless enough - or too hurt to harm me at least. My jumping threw the dog into a frenzy. Feeling more trapped, it began to bark quietly but excessively. The sharp yips rang out of the dog like an alarm whaling away.

I sighed, knowing that the dog would put up a fight if I tried to help it. As it was, the poor thing was in an aggressive state with its teeth on display. I slid onto the ground and crossed my legs. This seemed to make the dog all the more afraid. I leaned forward and stuck my hand out, even though it was too far to touch. It quieted back again to only growling.

Beck came through the door.

"Jelli, you out here? What was that noise?"

"Could you get me some jerky or something?" I whispered.

"What are you doing?" From where he stood, he could only see me, and the dog had gone silent after hearing the door.

I nodded my head toward the frightened animal, not allowing my still raised arm to move. Beck walked to the edge of the porch and leaned to see the dog. Without saying another word, he went inside and returned with a handful of jerky.

He lightly tossed it in my lap and whispered.

"What's the plan?"

I raised my eyes, slowly, pouty face in action and turned it to him. I lightly shrugged and he smiled a little, nodding. He took one last glance at the dog and then at me before he went back inside.

I proceeded to roll the dried meat, small portions at a time, toward the animal. The first few times he cowered away from them, that is until he caught the smell. A few pieces later and he was walking to my hand to grab them. The dog stood in front of me, pressing his wet nose against my empty palm. He had finished the food I had, but he was still very clearly hungry.

I turned my palm upside down and patted his head. He leaned into the warmth of my hand and laid down. After a minute, after it was getting much too dark to stay out there, I stood up and walked my way around the porch. He followed right at my heels.

He paused momentarily at the door, and so did I. He seemed healthy enough - other than having been starved to the bones - to safely be allowed in the house. So we entered, one after the other.

Beck saw how the dog followed me and raised an eyebrow to it. He took another look at the dog in a better light and realized how dirty the animal was. I turned around, examining the animal again, and then looked over the trail of dirt he left.

I turned back to Beck.

"Would you do me a favor?"

"What?"

"Help me give this dog a bath and find it some food?" I asked.

He nodded. "I'll get a few towels and some soap. Get the dog in the bathroom."

"An Aussie," I said after the dog had been washed. I ran a towel down the front of my shirt in an attempt to soak up some of the water. "I'm sure of it." I could tell from her coat, a coppery underbelly and a black-spotted, gray saddle of fur for her back. I could also tell because of the way her ears stood, her size, and the different colors of her eyes. Now that she was in better lighting, I could see that one of her eyes was the dramatically Australian-shepherd-blue, and the other was a coppery brown to match her stomach.

She let out a light woof, proof of satisfaction to her current cleanliness.

"Hey, girl, are you hungry?" Beck asked her and leaned down to pat her head. "Okay then, let us get you fed," he said in response to her wagging tail. "Come on girl." Entering the kitchen, he pulled out some stored, dried out meat and poured it into a bowl.

"What're we gonna call her?" I asked Beck as the dog scarfed down the food.

"Girl?"

"I'm serious, we need to give her a name. Do you have *any* ideas?"

"Nope, none, but maybe the boy might." He nodded his head toward the back of the house, where Stevvie lay sleeping. "Wake him or wait until morning?"

I shrugged.

"It would probably be best to let him sleep."

The dog began to bark, hungry again, which woke Stevvie anyway. He came out of his room, holding his gun at his leg and with his face unmovable and emotionless, until he saw the dog. Then his face twisted with shock, and he tucked the gun into the back of his pants. It was getting close to being morning, the sky had lightened a few shades.

Stevvie stared at the dog, who mirrored his actions, curiosity and disbelief on both of their faces. The dog shook it off and charged Stevvie, her tail wagging furiously behind her. The kid flinched aggressively, but that did nothing to stop the dog from tackling him and licking his face.

Stevvie pushed his hands against the ground to stand up. He wiped his face, though it did little good for him as he and the dog were of similar enough heights, and the dog just licked him again.

"What is this?" He threw a hand toward the dog, almost accusingly.

"A dog." I forced the words out through the giggling that I was trying to hold back.

"I know it's a *dog*, but why is it... right here?" He waved his hands through the air.

"She's a stray. She needs a home. You think she'll do good here?" Beck jumped in for me.

Stevvie took another look at the dog and paused before nodding softly.

"What's her name?"

"You pick," I said.

Stevvie's face lit up, as he took his focus off of petting the dog, and moved it to my words. He looked back at the dog, holding her face in his tiny hands and staring into her eyes. He stood up, confidently and said, "Her name is Marie."

Note

We had gotten our first snow. It was just Stevvie and me at the house to experience it.

I walked through the door already shouting.

"Stevvie, you get your butt in here right now and grab a jacket before you catch a cold." He paused in the middle of throwing a snowball to look at me. "Well, come on."

He threw the snowball for Marie, and she ran after it as he ran towards the house. He sighed, as if my worrying about him catching a cold was the worst of our problems and started looking for a jacket. He picked it up and slid it on, drowning himself in the excess fabric.

I stopped him.

"Why keep that one? It doesn't even fit you."

"It's the first thing you gave me, 'sept a peanut butter and jelly." He looked at me and smiled.

The memory flooded back in full detail, the blood especially, and with it the curiosity. He started walking to the door again but again I stopped him.

"Can I ask something about the first time we met?"

He stared at me, confused, but he followed my gaze to the shirt showing from under the jacket and clarity hit him. He looked at his hands, then the floor. He threw his hands stiffly to his sides and gave one sharp nod.

"How?" It was all I needed to say.

"I was sleeping in this house. It was scary, and I was alone. I woke up and there was a man just standing over me. He had a knife." His hand slid to where his gun usually sat. "He was going to kill me. But all of the sudden, he was still. There was a gunshot, and blood was all over both of us. He fell, and someone else was standing there. Before they could move, their infection killed them. It all happened so fast." He looked at me. "That blood didn't wash out. Neither did the blood of the others."

"Others? Who?" I asked.

He shrugged, not breaking eye contact.

"Didn't know them." He turned and closed the door on his way out.

I guessed that Stevvie had been through some tough crap, but hearing him talk about people trying to kill him made it so much more real, so much worse. I couldn't move for - who knows how long. I didn't know why; I just couldn't move.

The room pulled back into focus, only after I made myself remember that murder is a normal part of the world now. Five years ago, someone with as many deaths on their hands as me would have been considered a crazed serial killer. Now, people consider this many kills lucky: lucky that they didn't have *more*.

I glanced at my hands, seeing blood that wasn't there, and walked from the house.

The snowball I threw hit Stevvie square in the chest and knocked him on his butt. Though it didn't hurt him, it did clear out the air from his lungs. He grabbed a big handful of snow and flung it back. I tried, unsuccessfully, to dodge the chunks of snow. He stood up just to fall over again with laughter at the sight of me tripping and face planting into the thick layers of white.

We played in the snow, flinging it in the air and at each other. Making snow angels, chasing Marie and things like that, until our hands were red and numb from the cold.

On our way back inside, I put my cold hands on Stevvies face. He squealed at the cold and tried to do the same to me, yelling about how cold his fingers had gotten.

We drank some tea to try and warm up.

"When do you think Beck will come back home?" He asked me, between sips.

"No clue." I said, it was the truth. Beck had just disappeared, nothing but a note in his wake.

I'll be back eventually. Do Not *come looking for me.*

It gave me chills when I read it first, and then again every time I remembered the note's contents. It reminded me of a time - so long ago it seemed like a different life... of how he had acted after *her*. I slid my hand behind my back and crossed my fingers far away from Stevvie's prying eyes. Hopefully the oldest Beck I knew would be the one to stay. I cringed - visibly - at the thought of the *him* that *she* made.

"Me neither," Stevvie said, looking into his cup, pulling me out of my thoughts, and shrugging. "Maybe he'll come back real soon." *Maybe*, I thought.

We stayed in the house for the rest of the day, as clouds and wind drifted in and dropped the temperature drastically. It was hard to tell the time because of the clouds, so as a precaution, we turned the lights on early.

The wind howled all night, which surprisingly didn't wake either of us. What did wake us was the glass breaking, followed quickly by the bulbs and then by the terror.

The wind was so strong that it moved pebbles about like they were frictionless bullets. One larger rock broke open a window, not one near me, but near Stevvie. The sound of the glass woke me, but chills ran through my bones at the sound of screams. I was in his room before I could think to move, a piece of glass forcing itself into my foot making me yelp, and he was using a blanket to shield himself from the snow-and-glass-filled wind.

I ran in, despite the pain, and picked him up off of his bed, ignoring the small cuts appearing along my skin. I got through his door again and set him down. It took some force to close the door behind me, and I needed my arms to be empty.

Not seconds after closing the door, a second smash of glass, a light bulb, caught our attention. Every light sputtered to a stop, the central power of the house... shorted.

We were in the dark.

My body bent, trying to scream, but no noise came.

Eventually my mind caught up. *The basement!* it hollered. The thought fully formed as I remembered that the basement was lit with the power of a separate generator. There was very little cross over; it could be unharmed.

I grabbed Stevvie's arm and pushed the door open. Glass, sand and snow all shot at us from every angle as we ran.

We sat in the bathroom, because it didn't have windows. Luckily my instinct about the lights was right. I kept checking our left eyes to make sure that the dark hadn't infected us. We got out safely on luck and luck alone.

A long time passed, past our hunger, past our thirst. But our fear never left, we kept checking each other's faces for black marks. Eventually the sound subsided, and the wind died down. When it was nothing more than a gentle whistle, we left the basement. We walked carefully up the stairs and cut into the kitchen. I went to let out the dog, Marie, who had gotten locked in Beck's room.

She used the bathroom in the yard, yipping as she trotted back to my side. We went indoors, and she sat at my feet and made a soft whining sound up at me.

"Hungry?" Both the dog and the kid's heads shot up at the word. A chorus of growling stomachs came from the three of us, so we ate.

It was starting to get late by the time we were all full. I went into Beck's closet and pulled out a spare light bulb. I turned off all of the lights, though they weren't working in the first place, and replaced the broken one.

When I turned on the lights, they responded, seeming somehow even brighter than before.

We spent most of the night cleaning up. We picked up as much glass as we could, taped cardboard over the holes and attended to the larger of our wounds like the shard that had been forced into my foot.

After cleaning the last of my blood off of the floors, Stevvie tapped me on the shoulder.

"Can I take this off?" He raised his right hand to show me the wrapping.

"Let's check and see." I said, untangling the gauze. His cut was still pink and had some healing left to do, but it had scarred over enough to be safe. "Yep, can't get infected, so it should be fine."

He smiled at the news. He studied his hand as if he had never seen it before. He studied the scar, lightly running his fingers along the line that cut the features of his hand in half.

By morning Stevvie had fallen asleep, unable to fight it any longer. He had passed out mid-sentence rambling on incoherently about something or other. I carried him from the kitchen floor, where the cleaning had come to an end, to lay him in his now glass-free bed.

I sat at the bay window and watched as the snow went from a gray to orange, and finally to a glistening white so bright that I had to squint to look at it. There was still a little breeze, and after last night's storm, I crossed my fingers hoping it would stay just that: a weak breeze.

Marie switched repeatedly between sitting at my feet and sitting at the foot of the kid's bed. She too, sleep deprived, succumbed to resting and took a nap on the floor of the kitchen between us.

The sun was high above the house. I was in a daze from watching the snow when Stevvie tapped my shoulder. This startled me, and I jumped a little at the light touch. He handed me a glass of water, yawned, and left to let Marie outside.

After a few minutes I could hear his little giggle and her joyous yips.

I went back to staring at the snow, in awe at its beauty, its brightness.

After a few more moments of this, I got up and got to work. I listened to my gurgling stomach and made my way back to the kitchen. Walking lightly, to not hurt, and wincing at every step, I eventually got to my destination.

As I cooked, the smells mixed in my lungs, making my stomach growl more. The food sizzled and steamed. It was a good meal I had pulled together, toast, oatmeal and dried banana slices. I set the table and poured some human food into the dog's bowl when Stevvie walked in. He took deep breaths, as if by doing so he could inhale the food.

"I was just about to call you in. Hungry?" I asked, setting the dish on the floor for Marie to reach.

"Am I ever not?" he asked, though it came off as more of a statement than a question. He slid onto one of the chairs, giggling, he stuffed forkfuls of food into his mouth.

"Slow down or you'll choke," I warned him after a particularly large bite proved to be difficult for him to chew. He swallowed the bite, it attempted resistance, and he smiled, throwing two thumbs up in my direction.

I rolled my eyes, smiled and shook my head. Before my attention fell back on my own routine of bite, chew and swallow.

Since we were down a person, there were leftovers. I slid them into the fridge, which hummed away quietly as I did so, and I saw something that grabbed at my focus. It was a jar of blueberry jelly tucked and hiding near the back of the refrigerator's contents.

I pulled it from its place among the food. My mind wandered back to when I gave Beck these jars: Stevvie's first night here, my first night back. When my mind finished running through the memories, I realized I had sat on the floor and began tracing the jar with my thumb.

A quick look at a jar of jelly and I got my ticket to a past life. I stood up and gently closed the refrigerator.

I waited until Stevvie had fallen asleep, then went to check on the cut on my foot. I went into the bathroom, bringing with me some clean supplies to rewrap the wound, under the sink was some hydrogen peroxide. I slid onto the ground and grabbed the bottle, pulled the bandage off, having to pause several times because of the pain and the sound of dried blood crunching the cloth. I had the bandage off, but I didn't dare touch the gauze tightly clinging to my skin. I pulled the belt out of my jeans loops, folded it and bit down on it. I grabbed my leg, closed my eyes, grabbed the gauze and ripped.

Shooting pain forced out a quiet, high-pitched squeak from my throat. But it soon passed, and I waited, listening for the sounds of Stevvie waking up over my heaving breaths. Those sounds luckily never came.

I grabbed the bottle of hydrogen peroxide and without thinking glanced at the cut. Greening around the edges, bruised and bleeding on the floor, the sight of it made me audibly gag. Wounds were never really my comfort zone. I closed my eyes again and tipped the bottle.

The pain was like liquid fire in my veins, tearing through my lungs in a muffled scream, burning up my eyes in the form of tears. The hand still on my leg tightened until my knuckles cracked, popping from the pressure. My other leg slammed into the wall, pressing the print of the tiles into my skin. My jaw tightened around the belt enough to leave deep bite marks.

Eventually, after the bubbling sound faded away, I caught my breath. I ripped the belt from my mouth and threw it at the wall. It landed next to my foot, which I then pulled off of the tiles. I let go of my leg and stretched out my stiff fingers.

I grabbed some clean materials to wrap it with and began to rewrap the cut. This took a long time because I didn't want to look at it. Hard to do something that you can't see.

I cleaned up my mess and stood. The freshly opened wound shot pain up my leg and I fell into the door frame. I caught my weight and I leaned on it for a moment as I gathered my grit to leave the bathroom. I went to my room and passed out.

When I woke, the house lights were on and Stevvie was tugging on my sleeve.

"Jelli, don't die. Not you! You can't die on me!" he cried out. The urgency in his voice sent a chill down my spine, and this vanquished what was left of the restlessness in me, and I sat up in full fight or flight mode. A joyous wail, which I assume was supposed to be words, peeled through his crying as he jumped up and wrapped his arms around my neck.

I pulled out of the hug and grabbed his face, wiping away some of his tears.

"What's wrong?"

"I thought... I thought you died. I tried to wake you up, but you wouldn't move..."

"Hey, hey, I'm fine. I was just sleeping," I said, trying to calm him. His breathing slowed a little, though it was still very much like a toddler hyperventilating while throwing a fit.

He pushed out of my hands and pulled me into a hug again. My hands hung in the air a moment before returning to embrace him, surprised by this action.

A few moments passed, and his breathing was finally even and quiet. He tippy toed to get closer to me and spoke very clearly, his voice unwavering as he did.

"I still mean it."

Neither of us had said anything, and I was honestly lost about what he was talking about.

"What do you mean?"

He took a step back.

"Don't die, please." Then he walked out of the room, leaving me alone with that sentence.

I ran up the stairs, chasing after him.

"I won't." I spoke calmly, but seriously. Without looking to face me, he nodded once and walked to the kitchen.

Of course I couldn't be sure. No one could, because... I looked out the window and onto the ever-darkening world... things happen sometimes.

I walked into the kitchen. Stevvie was drinking water, and I followed his lead and grabbed a glass. I took some little flavor packets from the back of a high cupboard and tapped the kid on the shoulder with one.

"What's that?" he asked, looking curiously at its shiny silver packaging.

"Put it in the water." Hesitantly, he took it from me. I opened mine and poured its contents into the water. Every grain stained each drop it touched. I gave the cup a good stir, leaving the water a dark, foggy purple.

I forced back a laugh.

"It's a drink mix. It makes the water more flavorful." I pointed to the drink mix packet still intact in his hand and took a sip of the - now grape - agua. He watched intently as I took a second sip. Then opened his hand, grabbed the edges of the silver, opened it, and leveled the glass with his eyes.

He watched the water, as if it might jump from the glass and run across the room, tipped the powder out, and the transparent liquid faded to orange. He picked the cup up, looking briefly at me for reassurance, and drank. It might have been a bad idea to give him sugary water, because he was bouncing off the walls for about half an hour afterwards.

Starve

    The food had been depleting rapidly, even without Beck around. Several weeks had passed, and as our food supplies dropped, so too did the temperature.

    Stevvie and I had packed for the trip we knew we would need to take, a few days before we actually left. The bags sat by the door while we waited for the weather to change its mind, or for Beck to come back.

    Though he didn't complain much, I could see the food rationing and lack of nutritious consumables was starting to make Stevvie sick. We couldn't put it off any longer. Whether or not the weather wanted us dead, we were running out of time.

"We're going today," I said to Stevvie, the sun nor the boy yet up.

He jumped up, started throwing on as many layers as he could handle wearing, and grabbed a bag out of my hand.

The wind nipped at the exposed skin of our faces.

"Jack frost"- more like Jackass, I thought, setting down the bags I held, so I could properly close and lock the door. When I knew for certain that the door would not blow open, I turned back around, finding Stevvie fighting with the wind for his hood.

I crouched down and pulled some pins and two handkerchiefs out of my bag, quickly zipping it back up to avoid the spilling of its contents. I tucked one of the handkerchiefs around most of his face and pinned it to his hoodie to hold them both in their place. I took out some goggles and strapped on a set to cover his eyes. Then I did the same for myself.

"Better?" I had to shout over the protesting wind.

His eyes crinkled in the corners, a smile, and he lifted his heavily gloved thumbs.

"Good," I responded. And we were off.

The snow seemed brighter than the sun and could probably leave us blind if it weren't for the goggles. In some places the snow was so high it went past my waist, making me need to carry Stevvie because he couldn't push through by himself. The constant change in the wind's direction frustrated me quickly, *pushing us forward just to switch and push against us.* I wanted to yell, but what good would it do? The only one to hear me was Stevvie, and he couldn't even do that half of the time.

We walked so slowly I thought that surely we would die, hoping that it would be by the cold or the ever-growing hunger and not by the night. But mostly I hoped we would somehow make it to the next stop before nightfall *and* before the cold claimed us.

Our need to survive pressed us forward ever stronger.

Namma ran out to meet us, glancing at the setting sun before helping us the rest of the way to the house. She showered us in blankets and fed us hot soup. Then, when our shivering lessened enough to hear over the clattering of our teeth, the questions started.

"What were you thinking going out in the cold? Where's Beck? Are you crazy, and bringing this little boy with you?"

"We're 'bout out of supplies. This is the last of it," I said, patting my back pack. "As for Beck..." I shrugged, rolled my eyes, and turned my face to the floor.

"Sweetheart, where is he?" A moment of silence. "Jelli!" Namma shouted, slamming her fist into the table and standing up. "Where is that damn boy?"

I moved around beneath the blankets and pulled a piece of paper out of my pocket to hand to her. She read his note and rubbed her palm to her forehead, handed the paper back to me, and began to mumble to herself.

"What was that?" I asked, pulling away his note and tucking it safely in my pocket again.

"He's an idiot, and a dead one at that!" she shouted, moving her hand away from her face and making tearful eye contact with me.

"Stevvie, you should probably get ready for bed," I said. He hesitated. "It's getting late, and we need to get going really early." I spoke the second sentence softer and looked at him.

He hopped down from his seat at the table and left the room, but not before putting his bowl in the sink.

When the room was deeply silent, I spoke.

"He's not an idiot. And he is *not* dead." My voice was stern and colder than the wind outside.

"How would you know?"

"Because I know him. If he wants to live, he will."

"What if he doesn't? What if that boy brought back everything with *her*...?"

"He - I..." I had forced the thought from fully forming for so long. He told me he didn't want Stevvie around, but what if... what if she was right?

"He... well you know... after you two..."

"Don't." I interrupted, the strength suddenly back in my voice. I lifted my gaze, which had fallen. "I know - *know* - he doesn't want to die, I've seen his worst. Lived it. And I've also seen him at his best. He doesn't want to die."

She took a half step back.

"Then why did he go? Where'd he go? And why did he tell you to not follow?"

"That's his business and will continue to be even when he gets back."

"*If* he gets back..." she continued.

"When." I corrected, angrily taking half a step forward.

Her shoulders hunched ever so slightly, but I noticed it. Her head turned slightly as if trying to break eye contact, but not quite going through with it.

"I've got to get ready for bed. As I said, we have to leave early."

Namma looked startled by the raw, sharp edge of my voice, though she had seen this side of me many times before, it was rarely, if ever, pointed towards her, as it was now.

I left the room without looking back. It might have come off as forgiveness for her jumping to conclusions and putting all of that in my head, but I was not going to forgive her.

I brushed my teeth so aggressively that my spit was pink with blood.

I wrapped my hands around the edge of the sink and leaned forward, having trouble corralling my thoughts. *He didn't... He doesn't... He* will *come back.*

I woke up, the lights blinding me. My skin was heavy with the memory of *her* blood. I had another nightmare, but I couldn't run from it this time. I rubbed at my face. It felt like my skin was burning. It felt like acid in my very pores.

The acid stopped burning in streaks where tears washed down my face. My eyes felt heavy, but as they closed, I saw her eyes - black and with a look that her blue eyes had never dared to carry - my lids shot open, and my posture straightened. The light bulbs were blurry through my vision, and a hot sweat ran down my spine. My neck and arms covered in goosebumps.

I ripped the blanket off and ran for the exit. I hit the light switch for the porch light and pulled the front door closed behind me. The air was even colder now without the sun, but I welcomed it because it calmed the acidic memory of her blood on me, her death on my hands and the flames of her grave. The wind beat my sweaty, sticky hair against my face and tore at my clothes from every direction.

I stood there for a long time. I stood there until my skin felt broken from the cold and wind. I only went in when I thought I heard Beck's voice whispering so clearly in my ear. I could even almost feel his warm breath breaking through the ice.

"You'll die out here. You want to see me again, don't you? Go back in and go back to sleep." My eyes opened faster than the gasp that jumped from my lips, taking with it my breath. My head whipped around, but all there was was wind and cold.

I shook my head and dragged myself on stiff muscles back to sleep, this time dreamless, thankfully.

I slept for what felt like seconds and then we got up and off we went, back into the cold.

The food and warmth had fueled us, and our walking was stronger and faster than that of the day before. Our hopes lifted higher with the rising sun.

Even with the warmer weather, and the newly discovered sun, the walk was treacherous. Though the cold clawed at our exposed flesh, my mind was elsewhere... *What if he doesn't come back? What if he can't?* The thought of never seeing Beck again put an icy pain in my chest that made the weather around me seem sweltering.

A small warm pool of blood moistened the sole of my shoe, though the cut was healing, all of this walking was reopening it. Journeys like this usually did wear down on preexisting damage.

Stevvie's hand was nearly fully healed, now just a scar across his palm. Even with gloves on, I knew it was some shade of pink or purple, colored by the lower temperatures.

The wind hadn't died off completely, but it had changed direction and helped to push us forward, now just a light breeze whispering past our ears and playing in our hair. The wind was light enough and the sun bright enough to protect our heads without the need of hoods.

We walked further through the blinding, barren wasteland, until eventually a small hill of reflected sun, so bright I had to squint even with my goggles, came upon our view.

We walked over the last few steps of the hill, and a black spot on the shiny plain erupted, the pep in our steps returned once again. The hill of snow fell further behind us until it disappeared from our views and our minds, and we stepped onto the porch of the second stop.

I slammed the door in the face of the wind. My eyes were blinded by the contrast of the dark house. I stood for a moment and waited for my vision to adjust. First shapes and then colors began to form out of the darkness of the room.

I turned the rest of the way around, glancing at the dark spot in the wood flooring. A ruined section, blackened and warped, although there was only a slight difference between it and the rest of the flooring. It still pulled my attention and moved the hair on the back of my neck to a heightened position.

I walked to the back room and began to hang lights. After everything was prepared for the fast-approaching night, Stevvie and I opened some of the food that we had gotten from Namma. I didn't know why none of us had fixed the lights in this house, but the thought did cross my mind, and I only wished I had the things necessary to repair them.

I sat on the other side of the room, and in between bites, I ran my fingers along the melted and re-dried wax on the floor. I leaned my head against the wall... My brain thought of the last night that the wax which my fingers now traced had felt real heat, here leaning against Beck on this same wall.

I opened my eyes, which had slipped shut, and they automatically ran to the dark spot on the floor. My head pulled itself off of the wall as a thought formed in my head.

What if, like that night with that look in his eyes, he hadn't gotten over her? What if he was worse than I thought... What if he left because he wants to kill? I shook my head, the sudden movement caught an extremely quiet Stevvie's attention. *I had known - do know - many people like that. Horrible people. But Beck...?*

"Are you okay, Jelli?" Stevvie asked, leaning forward, his brows pulling in. "You're extra quiet."

"I'm fine, just thinking. How about you? Are you doing okay?"

He squinted slightly, shrugged, then smiled and nodded.

"Yep, I'm good." He opened his bag and pulled out a deck of cards.

"That's good, kiddo -"

"I miss Beck, though." He frowned as he started placing the cards carefully in their spots.

I sighed.

"Me too." At that he nodded and started to mumble to himself, counting along as he moved the cards from place to place.

I woke up, skin sticky with sweat. I was shaking furiously. I rubbed at my face until it was hot and red, yet the feeling of *her* blood on me wouldn't fade. I kept scrubbing at my face with my sleeve. Soft whimpering sobs leaked out of my throat. I was loud enough to start to wake Stevvie.

I fought myself and stopped, not wanting to wake him completely.

I pulled myself up and walked to the edge of the hall. I tried to take some deep breaths and to stop my racing, pounding heart, but my lungs screamed, seeming to stick to themselves and protesting the introduction of air.

The nightmares are back. It hurt to accept it. But the fact that I couldn't hide from it, hide in Beck's arms, that hurt worse. He always knew how to make the nightmares and the haunting memories seem small and insignificant, not so frightening. He knew how to wrap his arms around me and protect me from our damaged past.

I leaned against the wall near the doorway, then closed my eyes and accepted the fact that this wouldn't go away so easily this time. *I am alone with her.*

I stood there until my legs wanted to give in. Even then I refused to move, terrified that if I even took my eyes off of the shadows lingering not so far from me, that she would be there. Infected, again, this time because of me. Those bright blue eyes overflowing with the same darkness I watched swim through the air in front of me now.

An image of Beck's deep brown eyes made dark and shallow, filled my mind. But I still couldn't move. Cold tears streamed down my face, creating a sort of melancholy melody of pitter-patter as they hit the floor.

The air around me was suddenly too thick to breathe. The doorframe was the only part of the world not spinning, and it held me up, keeping me from falling into an abyss.

What if he's not dead? But what if Beck *isn't alive?* My legs finally gave in, and I collapsed to my knees. My chest tightened and my stomach flipped, palms sweaty, everything shaking. I couldn't break the image of his eyes - ruined - out of my head.

I threw up. Chunks caught in my throat which induced more gagging, stomach acid burned my nose and ran down my lip. I wiped my mouth with my sleeve and the back of my hand.

A small hand rested so gently on my shoulder, but still startled me. I jumped, still trapped in my head. Swatted at the hand. Whimpering, I fell onto my side.

"Jelli..." My eyes cleared some and Stevvie's face came into view. "Jelli, are you okay? What's wrong?"

"N-n-n-no-nothing..." I couldn't get the words out. "I-I-I'm-f-fine..."

He shook his head slowly in response. He could see it in my eyes: I was anything but fine. Oh, so slowly he reached for my hand, worried I might swat at him again. He took my hand, then faster than I could think to respond, he pulled me into a hug.

"It's okay, okay?" He patted my head, still hugging me.

But what if it's not? What if I... what if I never get to tell Beck that I still love him? What if, like her, I never get to say goodbye?

... About Four Years Ago ...

I laid there under the comforter pressed against him. I didn't want to open my eyes, scared to lose this moment. Every breath he took shook his chest. In... his skin touching the tip of my nose. Out... his body moving away from my touch. I leaned my face into him. A light chuckle shook through him, giving me butterflies.

He ran his hand down my side, from my shoulder to my ribs, and stopped at my waist. He pulled me closer to him and with his other hand lifted my head off of his chest and to his lips.

A current of electricity ran through my veins.

His lips were soft and tasted almost sweet.

He pulled our faces apart by leaning back slightly. My heart broke a little at this; I didn't want to end such a perfect kiss.

He kissed my forehead.

"Good morning, my darling," he said. His mouth, still against my skin, his stubble tickled me.

"Shush!" I squeaked and wrapped my arms around him, pulling myself even closer.

"Why are you shushing me?"

"Shush!" I said again into his collar bone. "I'm asleep. It's not morning."

His chest heaved with laughter. The sound brightened the entire room.

"Okay, we can stay," he said, as if knowing how much I didn't want this moment to end.

He ran his fingers through my afro of bed-head. I could only imagine the contrast of the bright cartoon orange against his long tan hands. I pulled a strand of hair in front of my face, opened one eye and pressed my hair against his chest.

It was comical. Honestly amusing. I broke out in a fit of laughter.

"What's so funny?" he questioned at my hysterical outburst.

I grabbed two handfuls of my hair and pressed it against him, laughing even more.

He gently pulled the hair from my hands and pulled it away from my face, gathering the majority of my hair in the process. He drove his arm through my orange frizz and with serious and burning eyes he spoke.

"I don't think it's funny... I think it's beautiful." He moved his gaze to my eyes and my heart leapt against my ribs.

I opened my mouth to say something, anything, but he pulled his hand from my hair and placed two fingers against my lips.

"Shush." he said, mocking me, and a smile broke through his serious demeanor. My ribcage relaxed at the sight of that smile on his lips.

... Present ...

Stevvie refused to take his eyes off of me. I hated always scaring him like this: I hated scaring myself like this.

It has been almost three years since she died. Why does it still affect me so much?

Stevvie grabbed some stale crackers and some water from his bag to hand to me, taking the quickest glance at the reeking pool of vomit, he spoke.

"You should eat, you're probably hungry."

I forced the food down. Rejecting the offer would probably just worry him more, plus I *was* hungry. I'd been hungry for weeks. His shoulders relaxed when I ate, but he still wouldn't look away from me and how much my shaking hands rippled the water.

I took a long sip and my throat stopped burning, for the time being. I set the bottle down and folded my arms to hide what was left of my shaking.

Although the worry in his eyes had lessened, it wasn't entirely gone.

"Thanks, little dude. I'm good now."

He slowly nodded, but his eyes said, "You're a liar." And I was.

I'm not good. I'm a fucking mess, I thought, lifting the unexpectedly heavy bottle to take another sip.

After a while, I closed my eyes and leaned against the wall, suddenly very tired. Stevvie scooted to my side and rested his head on my arm.

The sun was warm and bright against my face. I took a deep breath, expecting summer scents, and gagged on the smell of my own vomit. I shot up. *The sun?!* It was around mid-day, bright and much too late to start walking.

I groaned and ran my hands through my hair. My moving around had shaken Stevvie awake.

"Oh, sorry..." I said.

"It's okay." He looked around, having the same sun-surrounded realization. "So, we're staying here today?"

"Looks like it."

A moment of silence.

"What happened last night?" He was looking at his hands, examining the scar on his right palm and comparing it to his left hand.

"Just remembering *her*..." My voice trailed off. *Too late.*

"*Her*? Her who?"

"Just someone from my past."

"She must have been really mean."

"What? No!"

"Scary?" he asked.

"No... why would you think she was scary..?"

He sat for a second, turning his hands over.

"Then why did you look scared? Who was she?"

"She was..." I sighed, not realizing I had been holding a breath almost as much as I had been holding in the past. "She was my kid?" Stevvie's head shot up at this.

"You have a kid?"

"No, not exactly..." He looked very confused and intrigued. He shifted his body to better face me and nodded for me to continue. "She was mine and she wasn't... I couldn't have kids, but Beck and I loved her. She completed our little family. But something happened... she didn't make it."

He put his chin in his hands.

"And she...?"

"She's dead," I interrupted. I didn't want to talk about this, but a part of me needed to.

He reached over and gently grabbed my hand. A simple gesture, but it said even what words couldn't convey in the moment: 'It's okay'.

"The Finish killed her. It was an accident. But Beck had to shoot her... And I had to watch."

Unfazed by the discussion of violence, he asked the one question which hurt the most, made it all too real.

"What was her name?"

"Sammy. Her name was Sammy."

Sammy

... About Two and a Half Years Ago ...

Beck and I had a house half full of people, and tomorrow we would set off to the second stop.

I locked the front door, knowing that Sammy was safely in her room, and climbed into bed. I was just about to fall asleep when I heard a noise outside. The sun wasn't down yet, but it had been a long day, and everyone else was already asleep.

I sat up as the noise outside grew louder, as it grew into a shout.

I grabbed the pistol off of the nightstand. Beck woke and followed my lead. I unlocked and opened our bedroom door just in time to see Sammy sneaking across the living room.

"Where do you think you're going?"

"Someone needs help..." she pleaded with me.

"Go back to bed. We will handle it." Beck said quietly, as he made his way to the front door.

I followed him and, ignoring him, so did Sammy.

Beck opened the door to a heavily equipped man, scrawny and seemingly pulled down by the weight of his bags. His shouts morphed into begging, a chorus of pleading cries, when he saw us.

"Please help me... It's almost dark... Please... Please don't let me die..."

Beck leaned back through the door to snap on the porch light. Though the sun still graced the land with its golden safety, we only stepped to the edge of the light's glowing beam. We reached out, guns lowered, to the stranger.

We encouraged him to hurry, the sun lowering further, and darkness lay only seconds away.

The stranger tripped.

Sammy, out of some kind-hearted instinct, leaped forward to help. Both Beck and I froze under the light. She helped him to his feet quickly. Our mouths caught up with our minds as we called to her.

The sun hesitated ever so slightly, taking a last breath in the sky before it left, taking with it the promise of security.

The stranger stepped into the light, but Sammy had paused. Her head hung low.

My voice failed me.

She looked up, a black mark covering her left cheek. She looked sad and terrified beyond words. The fear faded along with her beautiful blue eyes. A twisted look, a desire for agony, ate at her once sweet face, and blackened eyes now stared back at us.

She slid her fingers into her pocket and pulled out a knife. She turned it over in her hand a few times, then suddenly broke into a run. It had happened so fast, I knew the infection affected everyone differently, but it had all happened so fast with her.

I fell to my knees, she - this thing - wasn't Sammy anymore. I couldn't look away. I wanted nothing more than to avoid seeing her like this, but I *couldn't* look away...

Bang.

Her blood, warm and still red, passed through the thin veil of light and burnt into my frozen skin. Beck, shaking, lowered the gun and fell to his knees. Tears pulled through the blood on his face.

I couldn't move. I couldn't think. I couldn't breathe.

Beck was sobbing heavily as he moved the shotgun in front of him. He angled in under his chin and began to repeatedly slam the butt of it into the gravel. Wishing for it to misfire. The rustling from inside the house was drowned out by the sound of Beck's desire to be taken by fate.

"I - it's her fault... She was too slow..."

Beck stopped.

"What?" It wasn't his voice, though it did come from his lips.

"I... just... you can't live in this world if you aren't fast... She -"

Bang.

Beck threw the gun away and fell to his side. He pulled his knees to his chest, struggling to breathe. I could feel his pain, I knew it, for it was also mine.

The gravel took in our sorrow and our tears, though we had more than enough to spare.

We stayed there, fighting and failing to breathe, for what seemed an eternity. People came from the house, screams and questions faded away into a buzzing background noise. My legs and hands bled from hitting the gravel, but the only blood that meant anything was that which stained my face.

Beck eventually raised himself up from the earth, somehow...

I, however, couldn't tear my eyes from what was once our 'little blueberry'.

Beck stumbled over, out of view, returning after a moment with a canister of gasoline. He drowned her still body. He pulled out a box of matches, lit one and twisted it out between his thumb and his forefinger. He lit a second, stepped backwards, dropped the tiny flame of consumption, and collapsed again.

She burned.

I would have gagged on the smell if only I could breathe. I closed my eyes and the world fell away.

... Present...

I told Stevvie about Sammy's death. He sat and listened solemnly. When I finished, the kid stood, walked what little space was there between us, and hugged me.

I hadn't realized it, but I was crying.

When he leaned back, I saw that he, too, had teared up. I wiped the back of my hand across the side of his face, and as he did the same for me, we both chuckled.

We sat waiting for the sun to rise, and when it did, we left for The Camp.

Once again there was no wind, but the sun did hide behind a thick blanket of clouds. Goggles, bandanas and coats protected us fairly well from the cold. Even still, the day drug on. However, the sight of The Camp's concrete walls fighting against the blinding white of the horizon quickly put some energy back into our steps.

Without averting my eyes from the entrance I waved a hand at the guards I knew were hidden amongst the gray. It was almost dark out, and the air had an unsettling stillness to it. Though The Camp was alive and active, something felt off, something I couldn't quite place.

We went to the school and 'checked in'. As we did the strange feeling wouldn't leave me.

"I don't want us to be here any longer than we have to," I told Stevvie. The hairs on the back of my neck stood tall, and it wasn't because of the cold.

The grool-oatmeal-hybrid-breakfast was warm and filling and easily one of the best meals I have ever had.

I spent the night staring at the lights. I didn't want a repeat of last night, but there wasn't a chance it would happen, there was no way I was going to be able to fall asleep.

The sun crept up slowly, tauntingly, as if saying, "Yes, wait for me, you mortal fool." And wait I did. I heard Stevvie yawn and stretch, and only then did I move. My neck was stiff and I felt painfully exhausted. I tried to force a smile.

"Good morning, Stevvie. How did you sleep?"

"Really good!" He smiled back at me, but there was something in his eyes... doubt. He didn't believe my smile. "You?"

"Pretty good." We both knew very well that I was lying, it was written in paragraphs on the circles under my eyes, which only deepened further each night I went without sleep.

Something still felt off. Not off with me; that I already knew. No, something off with the very air of the camp. We gathered our basically empty bags and made our way to the cafeteria anyway.

Breakfast, again, was hot. They did, however, give us a few slices of fresh fruit, the very sight of which made my mouth water. My stomach turned over with joy at every bite and my body yearned for more, but all too quickly the bowl was empty.

As soon as breakfast was over, we got to work gathering food and supplies. We didn't stay long, didn't stay to 'chat' or 'catch up'. My back tightened further with every noise. *Something is wrong!*

In no time at all we were 'checking out'. She wasn't there, the sweet familiar face of the teacher. Instead, a dull and monotone-voiced man spoke to us.

I left, not quite running, but definitely nothing slow. Stevvie did have to run to keep up. When we were out of earshot of the walls he spoke to me.

"You're scaring me. What's wrong?"

My steps slowed.

"I don't know, something just felt off."

"Because of the other night?" he asked.

"No..." I came to a stop for a moment, shook my head then continued walking. "Something else that I can't quite place my finger on."

"Right here?" He touched the back of his neck. "The pokies?"

"You felt it too?" I questioned him.

He nodded.

"I think it's just the cold." He breathed out heavily to prove his point as his breath formed a sort of cloud around him.

I mumbled, eyeing The Camp as it shrank.

"I don't."

The bags were heavy but felt as light as paper compared to the weight of the snow we pushed through. We got to the house late. It still wreaked from the puddle of vomit, so we did our best to hold our breath and wait out the night.

Acceptance

Another long day of walking through the grueling cold left us at Namma's front door. I didn't want to knock. If the dark wasn't a problem I would have just kept going, but the darkness was a problem quickly approaching, and I had Stevvie to watch out for, who was just as quickly running out of steam as we were running out of daylight.

He is so tough that sometimes I forget that he is only a child, some would still consider him a tiny kid. Most everyone *now* would either consider him a miracle or a dead thing walking. But Stevvie *had* kept himself alive, and not by some miracle: it was simply his determination that kept him alive.

I hadn't realized how long we had been standing just staring at the door, until Stevvie let out a long, shiver-interrupted sigh. He jogged past me and knocked on the door. Almost immediately the door was opened, Namma's wrinkled face switching from sour to sweet at the sight of the little kid.

"Oh, come on in, before you catch your death."

I mumbled a 'Thanks' as I passed her. I veered off to the living room and dropped my bags on one of the many empty cots.

It felt amazing to kick off my shoes. If I couldn't see my toes all there in front of me, I would have bet a thousand dollars that I had lost at least a few to frostbite. But no, there they were: cold, yet intact.

Namma came in not much later, carrying several large chunks of wood. For an older and smaller woman she was surprisingly strong. Behind her, Stevvie waddled in, struggling to hold his share of the load of wood. *Cute*, I thought.

Namma quietly started a fire, stood up, dusted off her floral dress, and left the room. At the doorway, without looking, she paused and spoke to me.

"Jelli, may I talk with you?" Then, she was gone out of my sight.

I rolled my eyes. *What's with the theatrics, woman?* I patted Stevvie's head and followed after her.

"What?" I was short with her. I had no desire whatsoever to hear what she had to say. I didn't want another argument about Beck.

She hugged me. Just whipped around and pulled me in.

Faster than I could react, she pulled me into a soft, grandmotherly hug. She whispered softly, so much so that I had to strain to hear her.

"I hope to God that you are right... I couldn't stand to live without that stupid- stupid boy..." Her voice caught between the insults. She really didn't mean them. She loved Beck like he was her own flesh and blood.

I hugged her back.

"I know. Me too." With that short interaction, everything was said, and any anger washed away.

I hope I'm right... I hope he is alive. I hope he's still Beck.

She stepped back with a light chuckle, wiping away tears as she did.

"Don't go tellin' people I cry, now. You'll ruin my reputation." I laughed and nodded my agreement.

I didn't sleep well. I didn't dream. All that was in my head was darkness: It was always hard to sleep when surrounded by darkness. Stevvie woke me by tapping my shoulder.

"I've got a funny feeling. I think we should go," he said.

I yawned and stretched, then gathered our bags to wait for the sun.

I, too, had a strange feeling. It hadn't gone away since it began back at The Camp.

With the first steps into the day, I realized, *perhaps this feeling... is knowing that I am* not *right. Beck is probably dead.*

Return

Stevvie and I had been home for about a day, maybe two. The time seemed to blur more and more the longer that Beck was gone. It had happened before, many times: minutes felt like years and the months passed me by like they were days.

Marie had been fending for herself while we were traveling to get food. We tried to bring her with us but she wouldn't go. She returned about a day after we did, maybe less. She had lost a noticeable amount of weight, but she recognized us immediately, and she seemed happy to see us.

It was dark outside, very dark, and laying alone in the basement was starting to feel almost like a prison. I went upstairs to Beck's room, and I found Marie laying on the foot of his bed: it seemed she had had the same idea. I laid down and pulled the covers to my chin, instantly feeling better, feeling closer to him.

Feeling safe and warm, I started to drift off to sleep, and then I heard a soft scratch. I thought it was just the dog wanting to lay in the living room, so I rolled over and pressed my face to the pillow, but as I rolled, I felt her on the blanket against my leg.

Another soft scratch and two light banging sounds.

I shot up and grabbed the gun out of the closet, my arms stiffening with how tightly I gripped the shotgun. I made my way to the front door, where I thought the sound had come from. I grabbed the door handle, squeezed it, and took a deep breath to calm my nerves.

I swung the door open, and Beck's head hit the ground just inside the house hard, the lightest of groans coming from him. *Beck...* I couldn't believe what I saw before me, but it was very much so real.

... About Seven Years Ago, in Another Life ...

It was after class, I was waiting outside my favorite coffee place, sitting in my car. I had the window down and could hear a chorus of birds, a sweet song to go along with the book I was reading. Law always was an interest of mine, so while others would fall asleep, I found the textbooks and lectures on the subject to be riveting.

I had gotten lost flitting between pages of the book and hadn't noticed my dear friend hanging in through my open window, staring me down. He stuck his hand over the page.

"Wow, Isabelle, you really do get sucked up into your own little world when you read..." He chuckled, and I closed his hand in my book.

He acted like I crushed his hand past the point of saving. He pulled his hand back and stepped away from my car. I rolled my eyes and got out.

"And you get sucked up into your own world doing nothing."

"Hey!" he said offendedly. "I mean... you're not wrong... but still, at least I'm not boring."

"Yeah, okay."

"Hey, so big news!" He often jumped from thing to thing, subject to subject. He was a very energetic person: he reminded me of a golden retriever in that way. I nodded for him to continue, and he did. "The court date got moved up. It happened yesterday, so I was able to see her!"

"What? Why didn't you tell me? That's great! But did anything come out of that court session?" I was upset, but I understood he probably didn't have much time to prepare, nor keep me caught up.

"Nah, nothing much, still fighting that fucking bitch! Like come on! She's my kid too! Let me see my own damn kid!!" He was yelling now. "Oh, we should get outta the street. Oh my God, I would kill for some good coffee." He was walking away before I could respond to any of the things he had said.

"Jay, I'm sorry she still won't let you see Nini. My offer still stands though, if you ever need any help, I got you," I said, catching up to him.

He put his arm on my shoulder, our usual bro-hug.

"I know. Thank you. Now coffee!" Once again, he was off and running.

... **Present** ...

It took me a moment to recognize him: he was so badly beaten and bruised that he almost didn't resemble himself. I dropped the gun and fell to my knees. There was no black on his cheek - other than dried blood and bruising - so I gently pulled his head onto my lap. Moving him made him groan again, and his hands tried to ball up.

I tentatively touched his face. I tried to fight back tears as he winced at my feather-like touch.

After a moment, I could no longer bear to see him in pain like this. I lowered his head back down to the ground, ignoring the knot in my stomach that tightened with every noise he made. I ran back to his room, Marie following in tow, I pulled the quilt off of his bed and went back to Beck. I laid the blanket down and grabbed the shoulder of Beck's shirt. I took a deep breath and pulled.

He was basically dead weight, but I pulled anyway, stepping back until he was on the blanket. I grabbed the corners nearest his head and started the process again. It was only a few moments until I got him to his room, though actually getting him on the bed was a much longer, and much more painful, process.

I closed the front door before heading to the basement bathroom. I grabbed all of the first aid supplies that were there and snuck back up and past the still sleeping Stevvie. Beck was limp on the bed. I couldn't tell if his chest was moving to breathe. I dropped the medical supplies next to him, and as I did, I noticed a particularly large spot of blood on the side of his shirt. It was still wet.

I tried to lift his shirt to see the extent of the damage, but it was caught under his weight, so I grabbed some scissors and began cutting. *He can get pissed at me after I save his life.* There was a large, deep cut on his side: I could see the muscle under his skin. He had lost a lot of blood, and there were many large clusters of bruises. I was almost certain that there was even more unseen internal damage.

But I had to try.

I sterilized the wound, and he shouted, though it wasn't words. His hand reached out and grabbed my arm hard. His eyes were still closed as he did this and his hand fell from my arm just a moment later. I waited for another reaction, but none came. I cleaned a needle and pulled his skin closed with some fishing wire. I taped gauze to him and moved on to the next wound that was most in need of my attention.

After a few hours of trying not to vomit or cry, bringing him pain in an attempt to bring him to health, I had cleaned him up fairly well. I had stripped him down the rest of the way and washed off as much dirt and blood as I could. I tended to the rest of his wounds, including one caused by a piece of metal still stuck in his lower leg.

I woke to the sound of dishes clanking against each other in the kitchen. I had fallen asleep on the floor leaning against the side of the bed closest to Beck and the door. I stretched, and went to stand but a hand fell upon my shoulder and squeezed it lightly. I whipped around, whispering Beck's name so quietly that I was really only mouthing it. His face looked like he was still sleeping.

I hugged him.

"Ouch," he said, very clearly through a split lip.

"Sorry..." I said, realizing I was putting too much weight on his likely-broken bones.

"It's okay. Worth it..." This made me smile, something about him just seemed like the old him. It was something, like a desire to live.

I wanted to stay there kneeling on the floor next to him for days, but I knew he probably wasn't like he was before Sammy died, and staying here thinking he was would probably only hurt me. I wished he was the old him, or at least that a part of that version of him had come back during his journey.

"Here," I said, "let me get you something to drink." As I left it looked to me like Beck was disappointed.

I stood on the other side of the closed door for a moment. Eyes closed, just trying to soak up the fact that Beck was just a door away. Stevvie looked at me funny for doing this. *He's alive.*

I grabbed a glass from the cupboard, and as I filled it, I told the kid "Beck... he's alive..."

He dropped his silverware.

"What?"

"You have to be really really gentle, okay?"

"Is he here?"

I turned and nodded to the master bedroom and began walking in that direction. Stevvie fell/jumped out of his chair and ran toward the room, too.

Beck was happy to see the kid, and to see me again, or at least that's what I took from his half smile.

"What happened?" Stevvie asked him at the sight of his wounds. Beck sighed and did his best to shrug.

I helped him drink some water, then ushered Stevvie out of the room.

"Let's let him rest." I wanted so badly to not have to leave the room.

Stevvie was asleep, and it was dark outside again, but I stayed awake because I couldn't go back downstairs, and I wouldn't interrupt Beck trying to rest. Both the kid and myself had kept out of that room, and Beck hadn't come out or even made a noise.

I decided to make him some food, mostly as an excuse to just check in on him and make sure he was okay.

I cut up an apple into small slices, and laid them carefully on a plate for him.

When I set the plate down, he woke and opened the one eye that he could. I turned, pretending that I hadn't noticed that he was awake, but happy to know he was still okay. He grabbed my hand and pulled it softly toward him.

I turned to him, and he raised his hand and waved it to beckon me closer, as if we were little kids and he had a secret he wanted to whisper to me so no one else could hear. I leaned in. Serious as could be, he put his free hand on the side of my face, ran it through my hair, and pulled me into a kiss.

Huh?

It was a very sweet and short kiss. Even though it left my lips tasting like the iron in his blood, it also left my chest on fire, stomach full of butterflies, and had me completely speechless. He moved his hand from the tangle of my hair and leaned his head back to the pillow, but he didn't break eye contact.

I was suddenly very aware of my hand still in his.

He spoke softly to ask, "Stay?"

I still couldn't speak, so I nodded, gently pulled my hand from his, and walked around the bed. I moved the first aid equipment to the floor and took its place next to him. I carefully moved closer to him, trying not to hurt him. I faced the wall and was careful not to touch him.

"Turn around?" he asked. "I miss seeing your face." I listened to his request and rolled over to look at him. He moved my right arm over his chest and said while gazing into my eyes, "Better." A moment later he continued. "May I ask a question?"

"Mm Hmm."

"Where are my pants?" he started to laugh, but he groaned at the pain it caused. I went bright red and went to pull my arm off of him, but he stopped me. "I'm sorry, I was joking. I'm thankful for what you did for me, really. I would have died if it weren't for you." His voice was raspy and broke as he spoke.

"Where the hell did you go? Why did you leave me - us - like that?" I hounded him, now that I had found my voice.

"I - I just had to go. I had to find something out there, something I had lost long ago." I didn't know what he meant, and it wasn't a good enough answer. I wanted to ask him more, but he closed his eyes, held my hand and drifted to sleep.

I laid awake for a while longer, listening to his thin breaths and thinking, *What the Fuck! We kissed? What? What is going on?* Eventually, I too fell asleep.

I startled awake to Beck taking a deep, sharp breath. I peeked at him to find him sleepily watching me. Neither of us had moved. He was still holding my hand, and I could feel his heartbeat against the arm still on his chest. It may have just been hopeful thinking, but it felt stronger already.

I had dreamed last night, I couldn't remember it after it was over, but I do know that it was a sweet dream. It left me feeling safe, or that could have just been Beck being back.

"You sleep so beautifully. So peacefully." His voice sounded worse than the day before, but it had more volume to it. The rest seemed to have done him well, there was more life back in his one open eye.

I smiled a little. I couldn't help it, and I rolled my eyes.

"Did you sleep at all?"

"Enough," he spoke, moving some hair away from my face.

He was serious, and even beaten, he was still so beautiful that it tied my stomach in a knot. I scooted away and stood up off of the bed, and he lifted his hand to stop me, his eyebrows pulled together from confusion, and maybe even hurt.

"I- uh, I should- yeah, I got some things to do."

I walked out and closed the door before he could protest. *What the fuck?*

I spent much of the day avoiding him as if he had the plague, popping my head through the door first to make sure that he was asleep before bringing in food and water. I was terrified to confront how I felt about him, and even more scared that he felt the same for me again. I struggled to help him to the bathroom in the morning, trying not to talk. He caught on quickly to my bullshit. In the early afternoon, I went in, thinking he was out like a light, only to find him faking. I set down the soup and water that I had with me. He grabbed my arm when I went for the empty dishes.

"I may look like shit, but it's nothing you can catch."

"What?"

"Sit. Please." I hesitated, and he softened his grip on my arm. I sat. "Why are you only here when I'm asleep?"

"I didn't want to bother you - I just wanted you to get some rest -"

"Bullshit." He cut me off. I opened my mouth to come up with another, more believable, lie, but nothing came out. We sat like that for a moment before he groaned, rolled his eyes, and began to speak again. "Do me a favor?"

"Sure...?"

"Help me walk to the bathroom. I have to take a piss so bad that I can nearly taste it."

"Yes of course!" I said, and we both began to laugh a little.

"Hey! Don't make me laugh, it hurts and I'm gonna piss myself. Just get over here please." We were both still chuckling as I got up and ran to the other side of the bed to help him.

I helped him walk to the restroom. He nodded his 'thanks', squeezed my arm, and closed the door to take a whiz. After a moment or two of clearly-someone-pissing sounds, the sink turned on, and then there was a thud.

"Beck? You okay?"

Another moment, bringing me anxiety. My chest tightened and my hands began to shake with worry.

"Jelli - I need help..." I opened the door to find him sitting on the ground, defeated. He did his best to make a pouting face. "I can't stand up anymore... I can't reach the sink..." I stifled a nervous chuckle and went to help him stand to wash his hands.

It took us quite a while to get back to the bed because of his leg, which I had to rewrap when we got there. The fall had pulled on the stitches and filled the bandage with blood, it needed to be replaced.

I went to leave after assuring he wouldn't bleed out, but at the door he asked once again.

"Stay? Please."

So, I did.

Stevvie had spent the day playing with Marie, keeping out of Beck's hair.

Another night sleeping so soundly next to him.

I woke up in the middle of the night to find the bed empty. There were some small spots of blood where Beck had been, but he was no longer there. I shot up. I found him lying on the floor face down, and I jumped out of bed to aid him.

I turned him around to face me. He coughed and half smiled.

"I tried to get up. I had to pee." I looked down to see he had pissed himself. His breaths were all labored and it seemed he had pulled loose a few of his stitches both on his leg and his torso. "This stays between us?" he pleaded.

I nodded and pulled his arm around me.

"Let's go get you cleaned up."

We made our way to the bathroom. *Being incapacitated like this must be extremely difficult for him, more so than it would be for most others. With his childhood being that which it was, alone like he often was, he has always strived for independence first.*

... About Five Years Ago ...

We were sitting up in one of the guard posts of The Camp. We sat in silence for a long time, with me watching the world outside of The Camp, but feeling Beck's eyes on me. I turned to meet his eyes and break apart the quiet.

"Talk."

"About?"

"I don't know. Anything. Yourself?"

"What do you want to know?"

I paused to think. What *didn't* I want to know?

"Who were you before the Finish? Who was Ethan?"

He chuckled softly to himself.

"Ethan was an orphan, he never knew his parents," he spoke of himself in the third person as if it wasn't his old self he was talking about at all. "He grew out of the system. He didn't have a family, but he wasn't alone either, he had one best friend who always stuck by his side."

"What happened to his parents? Why did he end up in the system?" He shrugged. "And what happened with his friend?"

"He got struck by lightning. I know, it's like a one in a million chance, but it was lightning that took him out." He seemed lost as he spoke so very slowly.

"I'm sorry -"

"It was a lifetime ago," he said, looking up to me, looking much more 'found' all of the sudden.

I reached out and took his hand.

"You don't have to be alone, Beck."

"I'm not," He replied, smiling kindly and squeezing my hand some.

... Present ...

I helped Beck down to sit on the floor of the bathroom. Then I ran to grab some clean clothes and some first aid supplies. We were rapidly running short on medicinal equipment. We would have to make a trip to The Camp soon, though I didn't know how we would go about it with Beck in such poor condition.

I helped him to get cleaned up and get changed. He seemed hesitant to accept my help, but he agreed after I joked, "It's not like there's anything I haven't seen already." He chucked a bit at that, which hurt him.

He was still in really bad shape, but most of the bruises were turning to more of a sickly yellow color: a sign of improvement.

We both sat on the floor together, exhausted.

"I'm sorry I left..." He was looking at his hands again, though they were empty. His head was down, so I couldn't tell for sure, but he seemed to be crying.

"Don't be." I closed my eyes and whispered. "I understand. You *had* to leave."

"No..." His hands closed and tightened into fists so tight that the blood left his fingers and his veins bulged up through his arms. Even his jaw tightened before he spoke again.

"I'm sorry I left you when Sammy died."

My head shot up and I stared at the side of his head, wishing he would look up- wishing he would look at me.

"It wasn't... I... you..." I couldn't finish a sentence. I couldn't say more than a few words; I had too much I needed to say.

After a long time, after his shaking slowed due to fatigue, he looked up at me still staring at him. He lifted his shaking hands to my face. I hadn't realized that I was crying until he was wiping the tears from my cheeks. I wished I could do the same for him, but my arms wouldn't move, so I tried to eb his tears with words.

"You didn't leave me -"

"Yes, I did." He sounded angry and he took his hands away from my face. "I did..."

... About Three Years Ago ...

Namma picked up the bucket of water and emptied its contents onto Beck. He pulled against the restraints and kept up his screaming. After a while he seemed to settle, lowering his head and calming his breathing. I leaned down to his level, and he immediately threw his weight in my direction. Started screaming vulgar nonsense again and laughing as he fell back against the chair.

I stood up sharply and turned away from him. I looked at De. "How?" I meant 'How do we stop this? How do we bring back Beck?' but he knew what I meant to say, even through so few words.

Beck interrupted him.

"You want to know how to *fix* me?! You want to fix me! Then *kill* me." I started crying and ran past De and Namma to the steps out of the basement. I had to get away from Beck when he was like this, I had to put space between us.

... Present ...

"It wasn't your fault." He started to sob at that, but I don't think they were necessarily tears of pain.

Spring

Months had passed, enough for the snow to stay melted. The crops we had planted were showing signs of growth, little green sprouts all around the brown between the fences.

Beck was doing well too, not entirely back on his feet, but much better. He seemed more himself too. When he smiled, and it happened much more often, it didn't seem fake. This was like my own emotional spring to see him smiling again.

Although things seemed to be improving greatly, we once again found ourselves almost entirely out of supplies. I had been pushing going back to The Camp off until Beck was healthy enough to go fast enough to not make us have to walk in the dark. I couldn't bring myself to leave him behind, either. Not while he's injured, anyway. I partially couldn't leave him for fear that he would disappear again.

We planned out another trip after Beck repeatedly assured me that he could keep pace.

The weather was still sharp and cool, but it warmed steadily as the weeks went on. The temperature seemed to drag out the days and slow our already snail-like pace. It felt like a longer three days than any of our trips before.

Beck walked with a noticeable limp. I knew it probably wasn't good for him to walk on his injuries like he had been, but there was no talking him into a bed-ridden rest unless he genuinely had no choice, and in this case there wasn't much of an option but for him to walk. I did, however, convince him to put his arm around my shoulder and let me help carry some of his weight.

For once, Stevvie was the one ahead, having to slow his pace and even pause at times to wait for us.

And that is how we traveled. It was a struggle to beat the timer of the sun, but we managed it well enough. There were two times that we almost didn't make it, rushing to beat that flying streak of orange that the setting sun threatened us with.

At the first stop, Namma cried deeply at the sight of Beck alive. She hugged him so hard she nearly broke the rest of his ribs. None of us got much sleep that night: We couldn't; we stayed up all night catching up on the past few months. Beck, of course, was still being vague about where he had disappeared to. He wouldn't give any of us real details.

The Camp still felt strange, but with Beck there, that goosebump feeling was easier to overlook. From our first steps past the gate, it was clear that he, too, knew something was off.

We checked in just as normal. Of course, anyone who had known that Beck had been gone was clearly shocked and even glad to see he had returned.

We turned a corner, and before I knew what was happening, there was a set of hands on my shoulders and my back was against the wall.

"Miss me?" *Clay*... I felt sick with anger and blind with rage at the sound of his voice, but before I could respond to his demand of a question Beck had forced himself between us.

Beck took a step toward Clay, forcing himself to not limp as he did so. Clay's hands were pulled off of my shoulders as he stepped farther from me. Beck continued to walk to Clay, moving him from me one controlled step at a time.

"You think I'm *scared* of dirt like you?" Clay spat at Beck. Unfazed, Beck took one large last step toward him, pushing him off balance, but Beck kept him up by grabbing his shirt. He, too, must have heard the slight quiver in the question that I had.

"Get your hands off of me!" Clay shoved himself away from Beck, disgusted. Beck didn't shift an inch, nor did he say a word. "Whatever." Beck only spoke again after Clay had crawled back to whatever hole that varmint like him came from. Beck turned to me and his voice shifted along with his demeanor.

"Are you okay?" he spoke with such concern that my anger melted away. He spoke as if worried that in that small amount of contact, Clay had brought me physical pain.

"I'm fine."

His hands hovered above my shoulders tentatively. I reached to pull his hands from their place in the space above me and repeated, with a look that said, 'I'm fine.' At that, he pushed his face into a partial smile.

"Who was that?" Stevvie asked. I had forgotten that Stevvie was walking behind us, blinded by passing thoughts of violence.

"Dirt," Beck responded coldly. Then he smiled quickly to himself. Stevvie looked confused.

"His name is Clay," I said.

"You guys don't like him much, do you?"

"No. But he's earned our-"

"Hatred," Beck interrupted me.

I shot him a sharp 'shut up' look.

"Mistrust. I suppose you could put it that way." Stevvie looked between the both of us with his eyebrows close, then nodded once, in acceptance, I guess.

Then his little cheeks rounded out to smile.

"Where are we walking to anyway?"

I looked at Beck, because I honestly thought we were wandering aimlessly, at least that is what it seemed.

"We are going to see De."

... About Five Years Ago ...

Beck and I were walking from the pavilions after another camp meeting. We were talking and laughing, about something I can't exactly remember, because we were quickly interrupted by Clay.

He stepped between Beck and me and started flirting with me in a way that clearly implied I was only some property to be claimed.

"Oh, come on, it's not like he can do any better." He threw a thump in Beck's direction. I stopped walking and stared at him.

"I'd rather choke on glass." I said after he wouldn't back away.

Clay stepped closer to me, and his once-cocky smile shifted into scowl.

"Hey man, back off. She said no."

Beck set his hand on Clay's back. Clay snapped at this, smacking away Beck's hand, then grabbing my wrist and twisting it to force me closer.

"Make me."

Beck shook his head.

"I don't want to fight you. Just walk away."

Clay swung at Beck and missed because he was focused on holding me still by my wrist. He let go of me and the second punch connected hard with the side of Beck's face. That fazed him long enough for Clay to get in a pretty good gut shot.

Beck stumbled back a little, leaning forward and trying to keep the food from the meeting down. He collected himself and stood up. He looked at me, his eyes growing fierce. Beck closed the space between the two and before I could tell he was punching, they were both on the ground.

Clay couldn't get a hit in. Beck, at the time, was smaller and maybe even weaker, but he made up for it in sheer speed. Beck was kneeling over Clay and pummeling him senseless, hit after hit, and when Clay stopped lifting his arms to fight back, Beck put his hands around his throat and started hitting his head against the ground.

"She said 'no'." He spoke through his teeth when he finally stopped, too angry to unclench his jaw. Clay was struggling to stay conscious. Beck's face softened before he scrambled to his feet and looked at me apologetically.

I hadn't moved at all, stuck in place by shock.

"We should get him to De." He leaned down and pulled Clay up and over his shoulder.

We hurried to the back wall of The Camp. Beck went into the house closest to the wall, and I followed but was starting to hesitate. The house was small, and I learned it was only to cover the entry into the back wall. The wall had been built hollow: It had been laid out as some kind of medical room or place for testing. Down a set of stairs and on the far end of a corridor was another set of stairs downward, but we weren't going that far.

De assessed the situation quickly and quietly pointed Beck to a cleared table. He turned back to what he was doing for a moment, then approached us with medical supplies in hand.

I stepped away for a minute. The smell of blood was making me nauseous. Beck came to my side. I didn't look at him, but I heard his steps come to me.

"How do you know how to fight like that?" I whispered.

"I had... a tough childhood. Everyone learns to survive differently, and I had to learn to fight." He clearly didn't want to talk about it, and I was overwhelmed by the information of the past ten or so minutes, so all I did to respond was nod.

... **Present** ...

We went to the back wall. No matter how often I had been there it still made me feel a bit sickly, just as it had the first time.

We went down the second set of stairs. De was talking through one of the many sets of bars to someone facing away from us. He heard us coming and turned to wave a hand of welcome. We approached.

The person behind bars was a woman, the kind-faced woman who used to help people check in. I had wondered where she had been. *Was she here, locked away all of this time?* She turned her face, and I got my answer. On her cheek was a thick dark stripe. She had been infected.

She smiled weakly and softly, watching as De walked away and we followed. Her eyes weren't black, so she wasn't in the second stage yet. I knew that the infection affected each person differently, but she had been missing for weeks, I though, *Has she been here the entire time?*

"You're still doing this?" I rushed to catch up with the surprisingly agile old man, questioning him quietly and gesturing to the cages.

He slowed.

"They *choose* to assist in the search for science. While they still can." He barely even mumbled the second part, but I knew he was talking about the second stage, when it eats away the parts of your mind that make you - well, you. He picked up the pace again.

When I first figured out he had been testing the infected he had told me, "They are already dead, why does it matter what happens to them? Shouldn't we take the advantage and keep others from following them?" *He is a smart man and a good doctor, but morally very sick.*

Stevvie grabbed my pant leg and held on tight. He looked so scared, that for once he looked his age. I set my hand on his shoulder farthest from me and pulled him closer as we walked to the end of the long passage. Many of the cages we passed were empty, but those occupied had people strapped down and stuck with iv's. Stevvie stared at each one as we moved, tightening his grip on my pant leg and shaking slightly more. *Maybe I should have made him stay outside?*

Beck waved a hand at me and Stevvie to tell us to stay back while he proceeded further with De. They kept their conversation very brief and hushed. With their backs to us, Beck pulled something small out of his backpack. De examined it, then nodded.

"This will do just fine."

Beck looked at me and nodded for us to walk away. He made a beeline for the stairs. I shared one sad glance with the woman in the cage before walking up and out of that room.

"What was that?" Stevvie's voice was shaking like he was trying to not cry.

"De is *trying* to find a cure," I replied. "He has only good intentions, I think." I whispered that last part.

"A *cure*?"

"So people won't have to be afraid of the dark," Beck jumped in.

"That can... happen?"

"Maybe?" I said hopefully. "It was like that once, maybe it could be like that again. That's why De does what he does. I may not agree with his methods, but I have to agree with his drive of pursuit."

... About Seven Years Ago, in Another Life ...

Jay had called me. His crazy ex had tried breaking into his house after losing the long, difficult custody battle.

I climbed to the top of the hill and knocked on his door, and his sweet little girl opened it. I handed her the blueberries that I had brought. They were her favorite and always seemed to improve her mood. She smiled, hugged me, and hollered to her dad. "Auntie Izzy came!"

I wasn't related to Jay, not in the slightest, but throughout law school he was always like a brother to me, and his daughter like my niece. They were a part of my family, so much so that I almost never called her anything other than Nini, referring to her basically being my niece.

We spent the day cleaning up broken glass and replacing all of the locks in the house.

"What do you plan to do about the windows?" I asked.

"Oh, I have a guy. Sweetheart, how is the coloring coming along? He's coming tomorrow and is gonna put in stronger panes for all of the windows. Can't believe that Bitch did this." Nini's response to her dad's question was a distracted thumbs up.

"I still can't believe you dated her," I laughed.

"Hey!" He looked offended. "She didn't let her crazy shine back then. I didn't know what I was getting myself into."

Good

... Present ...

It had been a few days. We decided to stick around a while longer than normal. Beck and I worked in the fields and helped with The Golden Garden, and little Stevvie got to play with kids his own age. It was wonderful to see the kid getting to just be a kid.

Beck and I had met a newcomer. His name was Zweety - like how an elderly woman would call a child, or a man would call his wife. He spelled it with a Z to remind him of the life before the Finish, his life as Zacharia. He was a large man, built like a truck and towering over almost everyone he came across. Although first impressions made him seem concern-worthy, but his name did him well, for he was sweet, like candy, in personality.

Stevvie came in the late afternoon to see us, tuckered-out from playing with the other children. We were getting ready to end the day's work, so he didn't have anything to do. He was sitting on the ground watching Zweety work when he pointed at him and spoke.

"What's that for?"

"What's what for, son?" Zweety paused what he was doing to indulge the child's antics.

"The orange spot on your shirt."

"This?" Zweety pinched a small orange patch on his shirt and lifted it to a better view. Stevvie nodded. "It's a part of one of my ol' jumpsuits. It reminds me of a life before this."

"What's so special about this 'jumpsuit'?" Stevvie prodded on.

"You get it when you go to prison," he continued after a short pause, and the boy's confused look did not wane. "Prison is like a big house where people go when they do bad things. When they are in that house, they have special rooms and special rules and guards to make sure those rules are followed."

Stevvie, now a little hesitant, questioned further.

"So... why did you go there and get a jumpsuit?"

Zweety chuckled, a heavy and jolly sound.

"Tax fraud." Another pause, "Don't worry, son, you need money to do that, and money doesn't exist anymore." With that, he went back to work.

After we were finished, we headed to the house we had been staying in.

I was laying on a cot, staring up at the lights. Half of me missed the days of sleeping in the dark, and the other half shuddered at the very thought. I assumed some time had passed before I zoned-in again, as the sky had become dark. Beck was up too.

I stood and walked to his cot where he was sitting, he looked up to me blankly.

"Hey are you okay?" I whispered, so Stevvie wouldn't wake.

He reached up and placed something in my hand, then without letting go, gestured for me to sit with him. I looked at what he had handed me. It was a keychain of a blueberry. I gasped ever so lightly.

"What happened?" he all but only breathed the words, and he began to shake.

"She was infect -"

"No," he interrupted. "What has happened to all of us?" *What* had *happened to us? Too much...* I took his hand in mine, placing the token of a memory back in his possession. *Not enough.* I tightened my grip on his hand, and he smiled weakly.

We sat like that in silence for a moment. Stevvie grumbled in his sleep and rolled over, catching both Beck's attention and my own. With this distraction and shift of attention, Beck moved his hand to my face and turned me to him.

He kissed me softly. I lingered for a second before slowly leaning back.

"What's that for?"

"There's enough shit in life, all on its own. I don't want to gloss over the good... You. *You* are good. The kid is good. Things like that, and I'm done walking away from the good." I didn't know how to respond, but he did. He kissed me again, then nodded to my cot on the other end of the room. "You should get some sleep."

I didn't have any words, so I took his advice and went to sleep.

His lips no longer tasted of blood, they left a sweetness on mine then reminded me of a different and better time. Beck and I had both agreed to keep things distant not long after he returned, but the way he spoke made me think he wanted more. *That would make two of us.*

... About Three Years Ago ...

"Do you know how old you are, sweetheart?" I asked the girl to try and get her to warm up to us.

She nodded her face, lighting up some.

"Eight and a half!" She seemed proud of herself to know the answer.

"And what's your name?" Beck this time. He reached his hand out to her, and she took it. He helped her to get out from under the fallen shelves of the library where we had found her hiding.

She dusted off her clothes, and I took a step back in shock. Nini... this girl looked so much like her that I expected her to say that was what she went by. But she didn't. She wouldn't. Nini was dead, and clearly this girl was not.

"Sammuel. But people call me Sammy."

... Present ...

I drifted off into a sweet, dreamless sleep.

Stevvie shook my arm to wake me up.

"Will you go with me to get some food?" I nodded and rubbed my eyes. I was beginning to get really sick of the food here, so even though I was hungry, I hardly touched what was on my plate. Beck came to join us after a short while, and he did the same thing as me, pushed his portions around in circles with his fork.

"I think it's about time we leave this place," I said to them both. "We should get everything gathered today and start the journey back tomorrow."

"Sounds good."

And so we did. We spent the day gathering any and all supplies we might need, that we would be able to carry back with us and readied it all in the house that we would be staying only once more. Although Beck was healing steadily, I worried about how a second trip so soon would affect him, and in turn affect his pace.

We would simply have to do our best and hope for the best.

The boys went to the house to get a jump start on some shuteye. I went elsewhere.

I knocked on the door and waited, Daultin opened it up to me. He looked tired but smiled still. He beckoned me in and spoke to Prince who was in another room.

"Honey, Jelli has come by." He turned to me and nodded. He pointed to a closed door, then he walked toward the kitchen and went back to the dishes he had been washing.

I opened the door slowly, peaking my head in first.

"Ah, hello there. Come, come." She was almost as sleepy as the little bundle in her arms.

I stayed for a short while, visiting. Soaking in the ray of sunshine that that tiny baby was. I even held him, having to hold back tears when I did.

It was like Beck said, we need to hold on to the good that there is, good like this little family here. Seeing the kid, although uplifting, also felt like a knife to my gut, seeing something close, yet infinitely out of my reach. I had always wanted kids; maybe being told I couldn't have any was why I so often helped any I found in need.

I got back to the house and passed out. I guess the day had been much more exhausting than I let myself realize, because the moment I laid my head down, I was out.

Someone touched my face, and reflexively my hand went up and out. I opened my eyes to see Beck laying on the floor, groaning and holding his now bleeding nose.

"What the fuck was that?" he asked through his hands.

"I'm so sorry..." I jumped off the cot and down to the ground. "Here." I grabbed his elbows and pulled him up. "You shouldn't put your head back like that." He listened but a little vigorously pulled his head forward, headbutting me as he did. "Oww, okay, now we're even."

"No we are not!" he shouted. "You broke my nose!"

"I - I didn't break it..." He moved his hands, blood rippling down his face, and looked at me like 'really, bitch'. I made a sound of disgust similar to a gag. He groaned again and covered his face, though it did nothing for the bleeding. "Okay, maybe it is broken... We should probably get you to De."

I helped him to stand and we walked to find the doctor.

"Where did you learn to punch like that?" His speech was muffled and wet.

"...You."

"What? When?"

"Watching you fight Clay."

He shrugged.

"Makes sense." He would have smiled under different circumstances.

We found De wandering around and muttering to himself like a mad man. He did what he could do to help, which wasn't much in this situation. As we were walking back to get Stevvie and our supplies so we could leave, I joked, "You just can't catch a break from the beatings, can you?"

Beck rolled his eyes.

"I can hand 'em out too." He began to throw a bunch of fake punches at me, pulling them back long before making contact.

When we got back, Stevvie was still asleep.

"How he can sleep through all of your winning... Tsk. I'm jealous."

Beck scoffed at my comment, and I shook the kid to wake him.

With the bags full and Beck's limp, we were slowed too much to make the trip in three days. The weather was kind to us though, warm and partially shady, we had grabbed a tent at the camp so we had a place to be during the night. We hung lights inside to keep safe from the darkness just on the other side of the fabric.

Namma acted like Beck was dying when she saw him again. *I wonder how long that will take to wear off.* She even cried when we left, though if you were to mention it or acknowledge it at all, she would probably put a shotgun to your face and say something along the lines of 'care to repeat yourself?'

Being home was a welcome feeling, and Marie showed up just a bit after we did. She seemed healthy, and she was really quite happy to see us having returned. I knew she could take care of herself - clearly - but leaving her always made me feel guilty. Maybe we can teach her to stay with us, so she can travel - long term - alongside us. I sat on the floor next to her and scratched behind her ear while I whispered an apology to her for being gone so long.

She trotted off when Stevvie walked by, and Beck came to me to help me to my feet. The kid and the dog went outside and started running around in the yard. I made us both some instant coffee, and we sat in the bay window to watch the sun set. *Ah, memories.*

"This. *This* is good," he said, either to himself or me, I really couldn't tell. He was lost in the world beyond the broken glass. "Add this to the list."

Stevvie and Marie came in, all out of breath. When it began to be too dark, they both went to the back room and quickly fell asleep. My mug was empty, but its contents hadn't done much. I, too, was tired, so I followed Stevvie's lead. I set my hand on the door frame, with its notches marking Sammy's time here, and paused before heading to the basement.

Beck set his hand on mine on the frame.

"Where are you going?" He sounded sorrowful.

"To sleep," I said.

He nodded.

"Obviously. I - just..."

"What?"

"I don't want to sleep alone." He sounded so innocent, like a kid who had a nightmare and couldn't sleep. He took his hand off mine and pretended to be all 'macho', "Sorry, uh, goodnight." He started to walk away.

I didn't like seeing him walk away. I didn't want him to leave me.

I jogged past him and into his room, plopping myself onto the bed. He came in and looked at me, somewhat confused.

"I don't want to be alone either." I smiled at him and rolled to one side, sliding under the covers. He climbed into bed too, leaning over to me as he did so in order to kiss my forehead.

"Thank you, really," he said to me before rolling away.

"*This* is good." He whispered. "This is perfect." I thought he was long asleep before I started to drift myself.

Summer

Spring went by with some light rain and a scattering of windy days. The crops we had planted were growing very nicely, and the spring-ready ones kept our rations from pulling too thin. Everything seemed to be going well. This made me feel uneasy and left me on my toes, waiting for the next big thing to go wrong.

Even Beck seemed happier, which was strange all on its own, a welcome kind of strange. I wanted to assume that this uneasy feeling was all in my head and nothing would happen, but knowing the Finish... I let myself feel this unsteady: I wanted to be prepared, if anyone *could* ever be prepared in a world like this.

I had been helping Stevvie learn to read and write. We all spent the spring living out a white picket fence dream. But like all dreams, you eventually have to wake up. This dream was shattered by a knock.

We most certainly were not expecting any company, and we didn't recognize who had come, but they knew us. It was a scrawny young girl, and she began talking as soon as the door was opened.

"De sent me. He says he needs the both of you, and that it is urgent." She looked between Beck and me. "You *are* Jelli and Beck, are you not?"

"We are. Jelli, go help Stevvie pack." Beck gestured for the girl to step outside with him, and through the door I could make out muffled speech. I didn't know why Beck wanted to talk alone, I hadn't known why he was so secretive with De, but I trusted him enough to let him keep it private - for now. I went to the back room to find Stevvie laying on the floor with Marie, trying his hardest to read to her.

"We have to make a trip to The Camp, let's get some things packed up, okay?"

"Okay." He hopped up and began stuffing things into his duffel bag only pausing to ask me questions. "Why are we going? Can Marie come with us this time? She gets lonely when we leave her."

"I don't know 'why' we are going, just that De said he needs us." I walked to him and gave him a quick hug. "Of course she can come with us. We wouldn't want her to get lonely, now, would we?" I went to my room to pack for Beck and myself.

"Nope," he called, smiling at me as I left the room.

I rushed to pack, then dropped both of our bags in the entryway. I went to grab the handle, pausing before touching it and running to the bathroom. I grabbed Beck's favorite knife off of the back of the sink, where he had left it when he shaved last, and slid it into my back pocket. He hated going anywhere without it; it meant too much to him to not take it with.

When I got back to the living room, Stevvie was already waiting for me. I picked up the other bags, and we met Beck on the porch. The girl ushered us into a car. *How did we not hear it pull up?* We all climbed in, and Stevvie left the door open. He patted his leg, and Marie jumped up to join us. The car was moving before the kid could fully close the door, and Beck reached around him and shut it for him.

Walking everywhere really made me appreciate vehicles. Hell, it even made me miss traffic. The only upside was that my legs never looked this good before the Finish.

The car ride was miserable with the dog's hot death-breath, but soon enough, we were approaching the gates of the seventy first camp of the North American region when I caught a glimpse of one of the guards on look-out. I was reminded of my time spent on those small walls.

I sighed.

"It's always something with De. Wonder what it is now?"

Beck let out half of a chuckle.

"One way to find out..."

"He said you would know where to find him when you get here...?" The girl's voice was frail and suited her small stature.

Beck and I shared a look.

"We do," we both said.

"Okay, then I'll just go check you all in." She leaned back into the car to pull out the keys and walked off in the direction of the school.

"Stevvie, how about you go and introduce Marie to the friends you made last time?"

He nodded, adjusted the weight of the duffle bag on his shoulder, and turned to look around for people he knew.

"Don't worry, we shouldn't be too long. We'll come find you when we're done."

"Back wall?" It wasn't a question, even though he seemed to pose it like one, and we moved to seek out De. Beck was right; the doctor was within the back wall, the lower level - unfortunately for us all.

De had this frightening crazed glint to his eyes. He looked through us like we weren't there at first, but when he saw us, he stalked toward us. Beck stepped back a little, limping and wincing because of a wound once there.

"I have found it..." De smiled, and his eyes widened grossly. He grabbed Beck's face and kissed the air in front of him before turning and walking back to where he stood before.

Beck and I both nervously, cautiously inched closer to him.

"Found... what?" I asked, scared for him to answer.

"I," he turned to us, holding a collection of things this time. "Have found the cure."

"What?" Beck's voice was stiff and serious. He grabbed the old man to keep him from turning away again.

"Well, close enough." De pulled from Beck's grip and started to walk off.

"You crazy bastard! 'Close enough'? What the fuck is that supposed to mean!" Beck chased after him screaming. Beck always gets his hopes up when it comes to this crazy old man, either he knows something the rest of us don't, or he refuses to accept what we *do* know. I, however, gave up on De's ramblings years ago. He was a good doctor, but simply a mad man.

De stopped sharp, whipped around, shifting the things he held so he could scold Beck with the waving of one of his boney fingers.

"You listen here boy..." he whispered, but even from back where I stood it was clear and bone-chilling.

Beck swallowed and leaned back a little, but he did his best to not look frightened.

"I have spent a *lifetime*," Perhaps he only meant it felt like one. "Working on this." He pulled some hair off of his forehead and took a breath to calm his rage. It didn't do much. "If anyone gets to be upset about 'close enough,' it is *me*." He took a quick step closer to Beck. This threw him off balance and onto his ass. "If anyone gets to say that 'close enough' is good enough, it is *me*. Understood, boy?" Beck nodded. He wouldn't have been able to speak with De looming over him like he was, no one would.

"So, what does 'close enough' mean, if you don't mind me asking?" I had to shift his focus off of Beck somehow.

He looked up at me and waited. His face slowly relaxed, and his eyes softened.

"I can't prevent infection, not yet at least. The darkness is still a plague to us all. I can't cure it after someone has been infected. Hell, I can't even stop the progression of the stages. But... I have finally figured out how to slow it."

"Slow it?" Beck sounded like someone challenging authority when he said this, his voice was steady and defiant.

Angry again, De turned back to him. "Yes. Slow it. Give those that are damned *years* rather than just days." I could have sworn Beck gasped a little at this, I couldn't be too sure; it might have only been my own gasp that I heard.

I ran to the both of them and lightly hugged De, making sure not to squish anything he was holding, and kissed the top of his head. He seemed shocked by the kindness. I let go of him and helped Beck onto his feet. It may not seem like much, but time isn't guaranteed, especially not in the Finish. Before this, the idea of infection and the dark were permanent, now they were ever so slightly less so.

Looking at the ground, Beck whispered.

"I'm sorry." De seemed to know exactly what the apology was for. I just assumed it was for acting disrespectfully, but something between them made me think otherwise.

De waved his hand in the direction of the stairs.

"Leave me now; I need to think. But don't leave The Camp. I will call when I need you again." He turned back to his things and we made our way past the wall of cages. "You two, don't say a word of this to anyone."

We both mumbled our agreement and ascended the stairs. I caught one last glimpse of the woman as we passed. I would have thought she was dead. She was so still, but her chest lifted and sank a little, and her eyes flitted beneath their lids.

We went to go find Stevvie, which was much harder than we originally thought. Although he wasn't a particularly short child, he still was a child, and they tended to not fall at the average adult's eye level. Eventually we found Marie, and she led us to him.

"We should figure out where we're staying," Beck suggested. "It's getting late."

We all went to the school. The grumpy woman who had taken over the checking-in station gave us a house number, and we settled in. Stevvie was worn out by the other children of the camp and fell asleep well before it was dark out. Beck and I, however, spent the night whispering back and forth about the possibilities of what this 'cure' could mean.

"Do you think De would be able to make an actual cure, or even something to prevent infection from this?" Beck was so hopeful. It was a very good look on him.

"I honestly don't know... I think he *could*, but I'm worried about what he would have to do to get there."

"It's worth it, though. The number of people that he could save... it's worth the costs." His voice was stiff. "Any cost." I couldn't agree with him, but I understood.

Before I could respond, we were cut off by a scream. It came from outside, and the four of us jumped to investigate. We made sure to stay under the lights, but it was difficult as we had to move quickly to keep up with the chaos of murmurs and moving people. We came to the source of the noise and had to push our way through the ever-growing crowd.

Clay... I scoffed and squinted my eyes. *What has he done this time?* And then I saw it - or to state it more respectfully - I saw her. It was the scrawny girl who De had sent to retrieve us, she was laying at Clay's feet, dead, bleeding still from a wound in her chest.

"What have you done?" Beck demanded.

Clay turned to him, waving around a gun through the air like it wasn't something to treat carefully, like it wasn't something that could kill as easily as it could.

"I did nothing... She tripped. Went in the darkness."

Bullshit. She was in the light now, no sign of marks from dragging on the ground around her, I couldn't see her face, but I could bet all of my belongings to her not having black under her eye. There was crying from someone behind me. I turned to see Zweety holding an older woman back, he let her go and she ran to the girl, rolling her over and cradling her face. There was no mark, just as I knew there would not be.

"What have you done!?" Beck repeated this time with more anger, taking a limping step toward Clay.

Clay made a twisted shape with his lips, but before he could speak, his response was interrupted.

"Enough! Break it up, boys." We all recognized De's voice and shivered at him raising it. Even Clay, though he would never admit it. De stepped between the two men and silently assessed the situation. Clay grew impatient and pushed De's shoulder. He went to say something but was kept quiet by De's fist.

"Don't," he spoke down to Clay, now on the ground. "You're out. At sunrise you will go, and you will not return. If you do, you will be put down like the disobedient mutt you are. I will make sure of it myself, if I must." De didn't seem too frightening. He was old, frail even, but we all knew he could and would kill Clay.

"What? That's shit! I have done nothing." Clay spat the words and lied through his teeth. De simply raised his hand to him, looking elsewhere as if Clay wasn't worth his vision. They were there for only a short moment before De walked away. As he did, he brushed his palm over Beck's shoulder.

When I looked at Beck, I saw that his eyes were wide, whether it was from De forcing the bastard out of The Camp or from the touch, I knew not.

Someone brought out a blanket to lay on the dead girl. The older woman's cries grew even stronger as a few of the people from the crowd wrapped her still body in it. She wasn't a child, but she was still very young. Even in the Finish, she had so much more life to live.

I went to the older woman, knelt by her, now alone as the people had carried the girl off to be buried in the morning. I took her hands in mine, and she looked up to me from the ground. Her eyes were red and lost, her face was soaked and shiny under the lights.

"What was her name?" I couldn't help but feel guilty that I hadn't asked the girl for it herself, while I still had the chance.

"Able. But that's only because - before all this - she used to say 'I am little, but I am able,' and -" she started to cry even harder.

"May I ask what her name was before the Finish?"

"Amanda," she choked out the answer before pulling me into a hug. We sat there for a while, I don't know how long, but eventually, one of the woman's friends came to get her.

As she was walking away I asked for her name, and without turning back she said, "Amanda as well, in both worlds. it was a tradition, once." And she was gone.

I continued to sit there, this time completely alone. I was too tired to stand. I couldn't help but look at the blood soaked dirt and think of the similar marking of the dead on the floor of the stop closest to The Camp.

How many more places like that are there, where only some dried blood, scratches or bullet holes show proof of a life that once thrived? How many of us have caused those, but be absolved of all wrong simply because the life we took was infected and intended to die anyway?

There was a hand on my shoulder. It startled me out of my dire thoughts, it was Stevvie.

"What are you doing sitting on the ground?" his voice was a pleasant sound breaking through the night's events.

"I just don't feel like getting up, I guess."

He nodded.

"Do you feel like company?" I tapped the ground next to me and he joined me in my solitude.

"What was it like *before* the Finish?" he asked, drawing shapes in the dirt with his finger. He didn't seem too shocked by what had happened, mostly he just seemed saddened by what he had seen.

"It was... different, very different. There were a lot more people, everyone had jobs and cars, and everyone complained about every little thing in their lives." Stevvie smiled and thanked me, it wasn't much of an explanation, but he never knew of the world before, so any information meant so much to him.

A silence followed. It wasn't awkward, and now that the kid was here, it wasn't suffocatingly lonely either. Beck found us like this, after helping move the dead girl. He found us drawing in the dirt, sitting in silence under the lights.

"So, what's all this about? Leaving me out of the fun?" he asked, trying to be sarcastic to raise the heavy mood.

"Yep," Stevvie said, smiling. He patted the ground but Beck simply shook his head and reached out his hands to us. We took his help and stood to join him. We all walked slowly, like our bones had been replaced with cement, but after some time we were back at our temporary house.

How long will De 'insist' on us staying here before he decides we aren't of any use to him? I thought while falling deeply to sleep.

... First Winter ...

The Camp was still a bit of a mess as we developed it, but with the first winter of the Finish, the camp completely fell apart.

There was little to no food, and many people starved. For one moment, the darkness wasn't what scared us above all else: We feared that none of us would live to see another warm day.

We did our best to stay warm in our houses, but even indoors, the cold burned our skin until we wished to lay in the snow and ice outside simply to escape the flames of our own flesh.

A few people decided to go out with the cold, peaceful and consuming as it was. They thought it would be better than letting hunger take them. Hunger makes people dangerous, the cold just pulls at them, makes them sleepy, and forces them to rest for one last time. People in The Camp thought it would be a more pleasant way to die.

Of course, there was always the harshest alternative, to die by the darkness, to wait while it eats away what makes you who you are, all the while knowing the casualties that you might take with you.

Every time someone would choose the cold, the few days following would force a grief over the people of The Camp, a grief so heavy it crushed almost as much as the cold did.

... Present ...

That same weight of grief hung over us all the next morning.

We watched, unwavering, as we forced Clay to walk. He knew it was futile to fight, but he still argued with every step he took, but his shouting was nothing but some whisper in a breeze. No one could find any semblance of mercy for this man. And so he marched to his inevitable death.

After Clay disappeared from the view, I turned to Beck to find some real warmth on this hot day. He was cold, his face emotionless and unmoving, but his eyes burned with something... joy. His eyes raged on with the pleasure of watching Clay forced to walk. I felt a bit sick at the sight and had to avert my gaze; I wasn't sick with Beck because I understood, I was sick with myself, for I, too, burned with the same joy.

The crowd gradually dispersed, but Beck and I stayed. I'm not even sure why we did, but it felt like we couldn't do anything *but* stay, like this moment was too long in the waiting to simply let brush by.

We made ourselves stop staring into the horizon where there was nothing to see but sand and sky and the occasional piece of rubble from a world slowly being forgotten. We went back to where we were staying - doctor's orders - and told Stevvie of what had happened. We were fine explaining it to him, but we had agreed that it would be best if he wasn't there to witness it, or to witness us enjoying it...

He clearly couldn't understand *why* exactly we both couldn't help but smile as we spoke of the morning's occurrence. The kid did, however, understand that that is how people in the Finish tend to be. They smile when talking of the dangers of others, just as that same smile also shows when some people hold a weapon, ready to kill.

Although time flew by, it was painfully slow to experience. Almost nothing seemed to happen all day, but still the day in and of itself seemed to happen.

The sun was starting to set again, and like clockwork, the lights turned on. As soon as the lights were on I began to drift off to sleep. I had a nightmare of something I couldn't remember, but even then I didn't wake up. It was a stable kind of sleep which tired people wished for. The kind of sleep which, honestly, I needed most at that time.

The second day, De called for Beck and Beck alone, which left Stevvie, Marie and me alone. We did some more reading, to pass the time, but neither of us seemed to know much of what was written on the pages, our minds elsewhere. Stevvie stopped.

"Will you tell me what your life was like before?"
"Before the Finish?"
"Mhm."

"What would you like to know?" I asked, he shrugged. "Well, I went to school, and had a best friend, who I saw often. I spent too much of my time worrying about things rather than actually doing anything about them. I didn't see my family as much as I would have liked to, even though I often *didn't* like to."

His little face rounded with a smile, so content to listen, even when some of it didn't make much sense to him.

"What is it like growing up and only knowing this world?" I asked him.

He thought about it.

"What was it like to live your life before this one? It's like that. This is all I know." *You're a smart kid. I guess only knowing* survival *has made you that way.* I chuckled and ruffled his hair.

"Good point."

We went back to our dull reading, again not paying any attention to the pages, only focused on the lethargic movements of time through the crammed-with-heat room. Stevvie's reading, and his confidence in unlocking the meaning of written-word was developing at an astounding rate. He really did have a knack for it, as well as for writing, though his hands would shake, so his words were a bit squiggly.

Beck didn't come back until very late. When he walked in he was tired, not just physically tired, but like he had been beaten emotionally. I asked him what De had needed of him, but he just shook his head, fighting off some kind of pain. I went to take his hand, but he pulled it from me and let it lay limp at his side.

I opened my mouth to speak to him, to find some kind of way to console him with whatever it was that he was keeping silent. I couldn't find the words, though, and so I simply kept to my own silence. So close, and yet an infinite number of worlds apart.

We heard a scream, again.

The group was there as it had been the night before, thicker in numbers than the last and harder to push through to see why it had formed in the first place. And just as the night before, the source of the chaos was Clay. He was holding Amanda, kneeling and still, by a handful of hair.

The same gun he used to kill her daughter was pressed against her head, now. How he was able to sneak it out of The Camp, I did not know.

I was focused on the woman he held, so controlled by the confusion caused by his apparent fixation of this woman and her child. *Why does he want to bring them harm?* But quickly my focus shifted. Clay had black on his cheek and in his eyes.

He was infected.

The group as a whole seemed to come to this realization just as soon as I did. Gasps sprinkled about the crowd and hands pulled up to cover mouths. Beck grabbed my shirt and pulled me back slowly, angling his shoulder in front of me. I hadn't realized, but he had done the same with Stevvie. He didn't fear this situation, but he did fear walking from this situation with one or both of us harmed.

Clay grinned menacingly and watched the crowd. His eyes were entirely black, but I could see the fluidity of motion as he watched us all. We all waited, doing nothing. I guess we were simply hoping that the infection would go to the third stage, and the solution would come upon itself. We waited, and it didn't. *How do we get Amanda away safely?*

Zweety stepped forward. Before he could do anything, Clay moved his gun from Amanda's head and shot him down. A second shot followed almost immediately. Zweety, and to the surprise of us all, Clay both fell limp to the ground. People rushed from the crowd to the woman and to Zweety, but I stood still, searching the crowd for the source of the second bullet.

I couldn't find anyone putting a gun away from the view of the public. That is, until I turned to look down at Stevvie. He had lowered the gun, but it was still firmly planted in between his hands. I reached down and rested my hand on his shoulder. This startled him, but it brought him out of the stupor that comes out of taking a life.

Stevvie put the gun away, took a breath, and then smiled sadly up to me.

I tapped Beck's shoulder and he shifted to face us, learning who had pulled the second trigger. We all silently agreed to leave and began to reverse our way through the crowd. Once at a good distance from notice, we increased the pace of our exit until we were safely behind closed doors once more.

We sat there quietly, listening to the ruckus outside. Beck spoke first. He walked to the kid, knelt, and set a hand on top of the boy's curly hair.

"Thank you." Beck smiled sorrowfully, and then stood to walk away.

Stevvie looked down, but he didn't look saddened or weighed down by the blood on his hands. His mouth was twitching subtly. It looked as if he was counting. And it dawned on me, he was. He was counting the number of lives he had ended.

"Stevvie..." He looked up in response to my calling his name. "Are you okay?"

"Yeah, I'm okay." His little shoulders tensed up, but his face appeared unfazed. *This poor little kid has lost so much because of the violence of this world. He will never just be a child... His hands will never be clean...*

I scooped him into a hug and squeezed him. I wanted to make him feel seen and feel less alone. He hesitated a little but hugged me back and hugged me tightly. Beck came over, knelt with us, and joined into our hug. We were all a bit broken, and our hands were all a bit stained, but at least we weren't alone.

Stevvie chuckled, all squished between us.

"I can't really breathe." He started squirming, making us laugh, and we let him go.

Three people lost in a matter of two days, two of them at the hands of the third. Able and Zweety... I would remember those names for a long time.

I didn't remember falling asleep, nor did I remember sleeping, but I knew I must have when I faded back into consciousness. Stevvie was still sleeping, and his brows were tightly pulled together making me think his sleep was all but restful, probably just fighting demons from earlier in the night. Beck, on the other hand, was wide awake, laying on his back and staring into the lights above him. He looked so tired I would have guessed he was just sleeping with his eyes open.

Tired but awake, and restlessly asleep.

The grief happened again strongly as we buried Zweety outside of town near where we had buried Able. Many of us stood helplessly at their graves, some placed flowers, and one person who I couldn't see was whispering what I thought was poetry. We all wished for something to do, but in life, any life, loss follows close in tow to gain. To gain anything, is to have something to lose.

I left before Beck or Stevvie did. They may be able to grow cold to the harshness of losses but I sure as hell needed a break from it, so I tried to physically walk away from it. I went back into the camp and began to wander about the roads. It was a still day, but I felt a sharp sting in my chest, the same ping of fear that I got in the dark.

I wandered about for hours. The sun had shifted positions in the sky drastically, that was how I knew so much time had passed. I was re-walking a street and watching my shoes with each step, when I suddenly ran into Stevvie, tripping over him and pulling the both of us to the ground.

Beck pulled Stevvie out from under me, chuckling softly at his groaning. Then he helped me to my feet.

"Distracted?" he asked me, but all I did was shrug and slowly start wandering again, still watching the ground. *Distracted? Distracted. Such a strange word...* My mind drifted. They looked at each other with confusion but wordlessly agreed to follow along with me.

Beck stopped me and suggested something to help move along the mood.

"How about we go make a visit to someone, maybe give them some good news, if they haven't heard it already?" I didn't know who he was talking about, or what the 'news' could be, but I nodded.

Beck took my hand and led me through the streets with purpose. Stevvie shrugged and took my other hand.

The three of us gradually made our way to the back of The Camp. Once there at the back wall, we went down two sets of stairs and to the first cage in the line on the wall. She was just starting to wake up and was clearly very tired.

"Are you here to tell me about the commotion from the last few nights?" She couldn't think of another reason for us to be down here, and must have been curious about what had happened.

"No, but we can, if you'd like." I said.

She nodded and rubbed her eyes. Beck told her of the lives lost, and when he had finished, she asked why we had come. "I don't know if you've been told yet… but De seems to have found how to stop the progression of the stages of infection." De didn't tell Beck or myself that we could share that information, but he went away and did it anyway.

She smiled softly.

"I know, it'll keep this" she touched her cheek lightly "from killing me, but it does take the wind out of my sails." He smiled back, a full and genuine smile, and set his hand out to her a few inches from the bars. She did the same. Neither of them touched though, careful not to, in fear of spreading the infection.

She yawned for a long minute.

We were in the process of saying our goodbyes when someone came down the stairs. "Do any of you know how to work the water pumps? They're having a problem!" A strange man with a familiar face asked. Beck had worked with them throughout the first few years of the camp's existence, he was resourceful and figured things like that out quickly.

Beck followed the man, and we did the same to him. Up the stairs, down the hall, but instead of going up the steps again to exit the walls, we went into a door and down again to a corridor full of pipes and large tanks. The stranger led Beck to the faulty tanks, to which he responded by dropping to the ground, sliding his hand under something boxy coming off of the tank, and pulling out screws one at a time.

He pulled off the bottom panel of the box and reached his arm up to pop off the front panel. The man leaned down to see better as Beck tinkered with the object's contents. Beck leaned back, full of silent anticipation, and the machine whirred back to life. He put the panels back in their place, secured them, stood up, and dusted himself off.

"There are two more that are having similar problems." The man shouted over the noise, pointing at a tank on either end of the row.

Beck had to speak loudly to be heard over the machine.

"Just do the same thing I did, on that one down there. I'll get this one." He gestured down the hall, then aimed his thumb behind him. The man nodded and began to jog to the farther tank. Beck turned and walked toward us, and we backed up further to be in the doorway, I didn't want Stevvie too close to the tanks in case something went wrong.

Beck repeated the process he had just gone through, though this time much closer and easier for us to see. We couldn't see what the man was doing down the hall, but we could only assume he was doing just as Beck had shown him.

We must have assumed wrong.

There was a clank and a bright spark at the far end of the hall. The lights flickered once and shut off, and the man dropped dead. The pumps shut off and it was only darkness and silence in front of us.

Stevvie and I were safe in the light of the doorway. The Camp was set up on many separate circuits, to try and prevent camp-wide blackouts, this left the kid and myself in the harsh lighting, and left Beck alone in the dark.

In The Dark

  Beck's back was to us. "Beck?" I shouted at him, but he didn't turn. He simply brought his hand to his face before his shoulders slumped. He pushed the ground to lift himself up, standing there for a moment, three partial fingerprints painted in black where his hand had been. "Beck..." I barely even exhaled his name.

  He turned and sprinted the distance between us. I thought he was coming to us out of an urge of violence, but I couldn't get myself to move, and before I could even see the color of his eyes, he had slammed the door in our faces.

  I could see his face through the glass. His eyes were still their lovely and comforting brown, but he was crying heavily. He mouthed something as I tried to turn the handle. Only after he had flipped the deadbolt did I realize what it was he said.

"I'm sorry."

My limbs failed me. I fell against the door and slid to the ground. I was trying so hard to think of what to do, but I couldn't think over the sound of someone screaming. The screaming got louder and harsher by the second. I wanted to yell at whoever it was to shut up so I could think of some way to help him.

I couldn't speak a word, though. I didn't have the air for it. I couldn't have pushed a word past the hands in my throat no matter how hard I tried. So the screaming persisted. It was a *horrible* sound, worse than that from Able's mother: it was a sound that pulled at your spine through every inch of your skin. This scream was a sound beyond any grief I had come to know the sound of.

My ears hurt. My mouth was dry and tasted of salt and snot. I felt something on my arm, though it didn't feel like it was *me* that was being touched. I turned to see Stevvie, his gentle face was contorted with terror, it made me sick to see. Only then, at the tear blurred image of this kid's face, did I realize that it was *me* who was screaming.

I choked on the sound, and the hands inside my throat tightened. I fell - in the newly found silence - to the ground. I laid there on my side, cold and empty, but I wasn't there; I was staring into the teary eyes of the man I love as he apologized for dooming himself to death simply to keep me safe.

I shot up, making Stevvie jump.

"Infected..."

I scrambled to my feet and ran like my life depended on it, because in a sense it did. *Beck's* life depended on it. I ran to find De. I needed his 'cure'. I found him speaking to the woman in the cage, and I grabbed the old bastard and shook him like that would somehow solve this problem.

"Cure."

I don't know what got him to understand what I meant exactly: the lack of Beck at my side, the tears on my face and the urgency of my voice, or that shaking him might have stuck it in his brain, but something did. He twitched his head in a nod and jogged faster than I had ever seen him move. He unlocked the top drawer of a filing cabinet and pulled out a few boxes.

"Show me the way," he said, and up the stairs we went. I kept tripping. My limbs were cold and distant and didn't seem to belong to me. Even if they did work properly, I could hardly see where I was going. Stevvie grabbed my hand to help guide me. My gut tried harder and harder to walk right through my spine the closer we got to the door, like it couldn't stand getting so close to Beck.

We got to the window, but Beck was no longer in sight. The lights had turned back on again - work of the backup generators. I leaned to both sides of the small window on the door to try to see more of the hall, first right, then left, where I could clearly see the man still laying on the floor. But there was no sign of Beck. De took his keys out again and unlocked the door.

De pulled something out of one of the boxes.

"We'll have to get close, but be careful to not let him touch you." He handed me a syringe-like gun and kept one for himself. He stepped back, pulling Stevvie by his shirt to place the boy behind him. He waved a boney, wrinkly hand at me, telling me to wait on the other side of the door frame.

He was putting himself up as bait, he had Stevvie stand a pace or two behind. De nodded at the door, I opened it, and not a moment later Beck was stalking toward the two of them. It was my job to stick him with the needle. I looked at the syringe in my hand and then back to De. I shook my head. I simply couldn't go through with it; I knew it was what was best for him, but just like in the basement after Sammy, I couldn't bring him any harm.

De's eyes lifted from the crouching and prowling Beck to me when I shook my head. Beck saw this and whipped around. When he did, De shot the contents of his syringe into Beck's neck. His face went from animalistic to soft, and for a short moment before he hit the ground, I could almost see my Beck again. I would have believed it longer if it weren't for his blacked eyes and the rectangular mark that ran down his left cheek.

De lowered himself to the ground. He took something from the other box and injected Beck with it, as well. He started to lift himself up, and as he did, he spoke to Stevvie.

"Go back down. By my desk is a stack of blankets. Go get me two, please, and hurry, son."

Stevvie ran to follow the instructions.

When De was steadily on his feet, he spoke to me in a much harsher tone than he had used with Stevvie.

"This." He gestured to Beck without taking his eyes off me. "You *will* explain later. But for now... If you can't learn to put your own 'sensitivities' aside, you will die."

I couldn't say anything. I knew he was right, I needed to learn to shut off and simply do what was right for the majority, but with Beck... it didn't matter the cost. To me, it was always worth paying.

Stevvie came running back with the blankets. We placed one on Beck and one next to him. We lifted him onto the second blanket by keeping the first as a barrier to prevent the spread of infection. Once he was on the second blanket, we dragged him to one of the empty cages on the level below.

"It can take as much as a day for the tranquilizer to wear off enough for him to be active, but he is in the second stage. I recommend not being around when he comes to. He simply won't be himself," De said.

"What? No. I can't just leave him."

"Won't," he corrected me.

I just stared at him. Once again, the doctor was right. I shouldn't be here when Beck comes to, but I also wouldn't leave him.

Stevvie and I went back to the house, Marie jumped and barked with excitement at our return. I told Stevvie to pack his things, to be ready to leave. He looked at me sadly, then looked in the general direction of the back wall.

"We're leaving him here, like that?"

"I don't know... but we should be prepared to leave if we need to." Most of the sadness washed from his face, but not all, and with each glance he threw at me, the sadness grew a little more. I could only imagine what my face looked like. I couldn't feel it, but I assumed it was horribly worrisome and getting worse.

I was in shock, neither my body nor my brain could fully understand the gravity of what had happened.

We finished packing our things, I hugged Marie and Stevvie. The dog wanted to come with us, but reluctantly stayed behind. We gathered whatever we might need to travel home and brought it back to the house. This took a large part of what was left of the day as neither of us felt like moving and we were dragging our feet thoroughly.

The sky was deeply in the process of darkening. We stayed under the lights and went through the door. I packed the new supplies in our bags. I stood and looked around to see if there was anything we had missed, and the only thing I could find was Beck's bag.

I had to make myself go to it. Clicked onto the zipper was the blueberry keychain Beck and I had given Sammy so long ago. I unhooked in and slid it into my pocket. Then I zipped his bag up the rest of the way and slung it over my shoulder. His things shouldn't be here if we leave: workers at The Camp will just clean the house and distribute his belongings to other people in The Camp or dispose of them.

"Let's go."

Stevvie jumped up from rearranging the contents of his duffle to follow me.

We got to De's 'lair', and I set the bags down by the entry. The woman was out of her cage, sitting on a chair beside the table. She waved weakly at us as we entered. I told De I wanted to keep Beck's things here until they are of use to him again. De nodded, understanding.

De pulled thick, rubber gloves on to put an I.V. into the woman's arm. He stood, set his hand on her shoulder, and he said something quietly to her that made her smile. He then turned to the cage that Beck was still sleeping in. Taking out his keys, he unlocked the door. When it clicked, Beck sat up and lunged for the doctor, held back by restraints connected to the wall.

Beck chuckled a little, not letting out the tension of the chains. He turned to me, his dark eyes widening some, and his mouth twisting into a malicious smile. I held strong and took the distance one step at a time. I stood about a foot from him. "Brave..." He whispered. Even his voice didn't sound like Beck's.

I heard the faint rumble of thunder, which meant lightning had led not too long before, but Beck seemed unaffected by the thought. He didn't seem to even hear the distant storm and the fear which would normally come with it.

I tensed my jaw but stayed silent and refused to move. De was at the entry of the cage with Stevvie standing behind him. The smile disappeared off of Beck's face and he groaned, stumbling backwards, and to the ground he went. I took a step forward, reaching out to him, He jumped back up and lunged at me, and I scrambled back just in time for him not to be able to touch me.

He laughed heartily and fell backward onto the bed against the far wall.

I heard a gasp behind me and turned to see who the sound came from. The woman was holding Stevvie, and she was crying.

"I'm so - so sorry... He fell - I - I didn't think..." She pulled her hands to her face and cried with what strength she had. *In false lighting... skin to skin contact...* Even my thoughts choked on the words. *Stevvie is as good as dead... at very least infected.*

Stevvie pulled himself up and away from the woman. He brought his hand to his cheek, touching it lightly, seeing clean fingers as he pulled his hand down again. He repeated this a few times, and each time was surprised to see nothing. We all sat there confused and waiting. *Yes, the stages affect people differently, but the first stage is almost always instant.*

After a second gasp, I turned to see De covering his mouth, then turned back to the boy to see if the mark had shown on Stevvie's face yet, but it hadn't. I looked back to the doctor. He whispered through his hands in a single breath.

"He's immune...?" De's lips went from open in shock to a twisted, wicked grin.

I knew what this meant. I knew what this meant through the eyes of De. Stevvie was the key he needed to find a *real* cure. But what he would have to do to the kid in order to find this said cure...

"No." I stood from where I was crouching by Stevvie to size up the doctor. "You will not lay a hand on him," I whispered sternly.

De's brows pulled together, and his mouth lowered into a scowl.

"The right thing. Do it."

"I am." We were speaking so very quietly, but there was so much anger in the soft sentences. Beck began to laugh again, but his laugh distracted the doctor and I seized my chance. When Beck laughed, and De turned his head, I grabbed Stevvie, picking him up and carrying him from this place before De could make him a lab rat.

De shouted after us. I ran like I never had before.

Staying here could give Beck what he needs... I would pay any cost to do so... but it wasn't my price that would be paid. I could feel my limbs again, for they had a purpose: to carry us both to safety. We ran beneath the lights. Almost the entire camp was asleep, so we ran in solitude.

I wasn't even sure if De would follow us, but I couldn't risk it. We got to the house and grabbed our bags. I was getting winded, but I had much farther to go before I could rest. Marie chased us as we continued to flee. The car that the girl, Able, had brought us in just a few days earlier was still parked at the front of The Camp. Luckily for us, no one had thought to move it with all of the chaos of the past few days.

I threw the bags in the back seat and opened the passenger door for Stevvie and Marie before running around the car and jumping into the driver's seat. *Where do they keep the spare again?* I ran my hand around the crevices of the vehicle, trying to find where they had taped the spare key in this car before the lights turned off.

The lights started to dim ever so slightly, but just in time I found it taped under the edge of the cushion under my seat. I turned it over in the ignition. The car revved to life, and the lights brightened. I sighed, pressing the break and pulling the car out of park. I whipped around, throwing dirt into the air. Stevvie almost fell out of his seat and into mine as I did so, and I paused and buckled his belt, telling the dog to get in the back seat.

"Let's go." Stevvie smiled, and we went.

We were driving for a little while before Stevvie fell asleep. *Poor kid.* Only when he was sleeping did he seem completely like a child. The way he held himself and spoke, simply the way he *was* made him seem older. But when he slept, the little kid was just that: a little kid.

We drove on and on. The gas was low, and I was concerned we wouldn't make it home in time, concerned about getting stuck in the darkness. I wasn't worried for Stevvie so much: he seemed to be immune, but I wasn't and if I got infected, then Stevvie would be in danger. I promised myself I'd figure it out, I'd find a way to keep him safe. *I have to keep Stevvie safe.*

We did make it, just in time. We sat in the car for a little while, trying to figure out how to get in the house to turn on the lights. Stevvie set his hand on mine on the steering wheel.

"Let me go."

"What? No! We don't know if you're *actually* immune."

"But we know that you *aren't.*" He opened the door and stepped out into the darkness. "See?" He touched his face and rotated his hands to show me clean fingers. He smiled and ran toward the house.

Even with the proof I had, I couldn't help but prepare to have another situation like that with Sammy on my hands. I grabbed the knife out of my pocket, the key chain falling out with it, and held them both in my hands. Trying to prepare myself for whatever may come about.

The lights came on within the house, and just a few seconds later Stevvie came running out through the front door. His face was still unmarked, and he was still not infected. *Shit... He really is immune.* He came up to the window and pointed to the ground. I rolled the window down, and he spoke to me.

"It is *hard* to see in that house in the dark."

He laughed a little. It was nice to hear that the events of the last few days' hadn't taken his laugh from him.

"I have an idea, so you drive the car up to the porch with this side by the light, then you don't have to walk in the dark." *Very smart, even I was struggling to figure out how to avoid the darkness.*

I nodded and smiled back at him, to which he ran to the top of the porch to wait for me. I followed his instructions and met up with him at the top of the porch. Before I did, however, I grabbed our bags and called Marie to come with me.

"Let's get some sleep." I said, ruffling his curly dark brown hair. This made me think of all the times I had ruffled Beck's dark hair. *How could I have left him?*

We dropped the bags in the front room, we all seemed to be hungry, but even more so, we were tired. It was empty and lonely to lay in that big bed without Beck, so like a little kid, I went to the back room and tapped Stevvie on the shoulder.

"Is it okay if I sleep in here with you two?" Marie's ears lifted when I spoke, but other than that, she seemed to still be sleeping. Stevvie, on the other hand, sat up.

"Of course," he said. "Just find somewhere comfortable, and there should be more blankets over there." He pointed to the corner before a smile turned into a yawn, and he laid down and fell back to sleep. I grabbed a blanket and found a comfy spot on the ground, then quickly followed his lead.

I had nightmares of Beck's face as twisted as it was when he was no longer himself, but I didn't wake up. I needed the rest too much, and my body knew it.

I didn't wake up until the sun was high. I sat up and stretched my arms out. Stevvie was still asleep, but Marie was nowhere in sight. I got up to go and turn off the lights. I made the kid some breakfast, eggs and bacon, I set some on a plate on the ground for Marie who had shown up to the smell of food.

I snuck back into Stevvie's room, tapped him on the shoulder and handed him the plate of food. He, just like the dog, began to scarf it down. I went back to the kitchen and ate my food at the small table, leaning to see the view of the bay window in the living room.

After eating I went to unpack the supplies we had gathered before leaving The Camp the day before. Putting the food in the kitchen, medical supplies in the basement bathroom, and the list goes on.

Although it was hot outside and hotter still in the house, I still felt cold. I took a shower to help, but it didn't do anything near much. It wasn't a surface level feeling; it wasn't the kind of cold that could often be helped. This distant feeling, I knew what it was, but I couldn't bring myself to do the only thing which could fix it.

I sat outside the basement bathroom, too unmotivated to dry my hair so it stuck to my skin and weighed a ton as it stretched down my back and shoulders. I leaned my head against the wall behind me. My eyes drifted over to where Beck had been for so long just after we had lost Sammy. I thought then that that was the worst I could have seen him- if only I could have known what he would be like infected...

I closed my eyes tight and pushed out the images. When they finally left me I was asleep again.

I had a good dream, of the world before the Finish. I couldn't remember it by the time Stevvie shook me awake, but it was something similar to childhood nostalgia, like remembering the distinct smell of chalk, rolling down hills of freshly cut grass and getting green stains along your clothes, things like that. I looked at Stevvie sleepily. *He may never get to have memories like that, nostalgic moments like that. But... maybe I can try to find a way to give him some.*

"Are you okay?" he asked.

I smiled at him and nodded.

"What time is it?"

"Not sunset, but the sun is kinda low in the sky." He responded, looking to the side to think for a moment before his eyes found their way back to our conversation. "Why?"

"Because I have an idea for tomorrow, if you're up for a little adventure." He nodded and looked excited. "Good, cause I think you'll enjoy this."

Chalk

   I was up before the sun, packed and ready for an adventure. The kid woke up a bit later than me, and he seemed pretty excited, although perhaps a little nervous. I gave him breakfast and he ate while we walked. I moved the car, knowing it didn't have enough gas to go nearly anywhere, so we walked.

   The 'adventure' I had planned was to go scavenging with the kid to find some chalk. I wanted to give him something fun to fill his time, give him a little bit of the childhood he would never be able to have. A creative outlet.

   We walked for a long time. Gradually, the rubble became more frequent, and that rubble began to change into buildings, which we searched. We went through many buildings. I didn't tell him what we were looking for, so he just grabbed other supplies that we might need. He was having fun looking at the situation like a mystery or a treasure hunt.

Finally, in what was once a child's bedroom, I found it. It was old and the set was used, but it would definitely do the trick. I shoved it into my bag when he walked in the room.

"Okay, we can head back now, it's getting late enough we should."

His smile faded a little.

"Did we get what we came for?" He sounded hopeful that I might say no, and that we could keep scavenging. I just nodded and patted his head as I walked past. He jogged to keep up with me, his little legs slowing him down as he tried to catch up.

We made it back to the house with enough time to turn on the lights. We went to the basement and sat on the concrete floor. I pulled the chalk out of my bag and handed it to him. He opened it, looking confused. I gestured for him to try it, but he took that as 'try to eat it'. He regretted that very quickly. I laughed fully heartedly, taking the peace of chalk from his hand which he had licked and slid it across the ground.

"Oh..." He laughed bashfully. "It's for drawing?"

"Yep." I said, handing it back to him. "Hey, you keep playing with these and I'll go make us some food. That sound good?" He started drawing and smiling. Without looking up at me, he agreed to what I had said. I finished pushing myself to my feet and headed up the stairs, through the spare room and to the kitchen to make some more food for the three of us.

Marie followed me step for step as I went throughout the kitchen preparing food, and I had to move to not step on her. At first, I thought it was because she wanted what I was making, yet even after laying down a plate for her on the ground, she still wanted to be right with me. I called down to the kid and set both of our plates on the table before dropping to the ground to pet the dog.

Stevvie hollered up that he would be just a bit. Marie seemed to understand in a way and rolled over onto my lap to get belly rubs. When Stevvie came in through the back room, Marie was trying very hard to lick the inside of my mouth, which I fought thoroughly. He laughed and pointed when I lost balance and fell on my back. I pushed the dog off of me and scrambled to my feet whipping her drool off of my face with my shirt's sleeves.

We sat down at the table and ate our food. Through a mouthful I asked him, "So, how is the coloring coming along?"

He hurriedly chewed what was left of the bite in his mouth and swallowed.

"It's really good so far I think, I like it a lot!"

"So you're having fun?"

"Absolutely!" he said, rounding his little face with a wide and toothy smile. "What is it called? I tried reading it, but I haven't seen that word on the box before, I'm not sure know how to say it."

"Chalk," I told him.

"Chaa-wk?" he asked me. "Then why isn't there a 'w' and why is there a 'l'?"

I chuckled a little bit.

"Sometimes words are just like that. English can have some stupid rules."

He made a scrunched face, kind of grumpy and kind of frustrated, but from my end of the table, it was more so on the side of 'adorable'.

"Can I see your drawing when you're done with it?" I asked before he took another bite to continue eating.

"Mhm," he mumbled before shoveling more food into his mouth. I went back to eating as well. When we were done, he had me follow him downstairs to look at what he had drawn. It was surprisingly beautiful, he had only used the one color of chalk, but he had some clear shading and variation in values. He had drawn in shapes and created a strange but pretty pattern on the floor.

I spared no expense in showing my appreciation of his art. Sure, it was that of a child, but it still had quality and personality. I told him all of this and gave him a big bear hug. He hugged me back, around the neck, unintentionally choking me a little but he had nothing but kindness in his intentions.

Trying to stay in the kind of feeling that this moment brought me, reminded me of all of those times with Sammy and Beck. Staying still here though made me antsy that I couldn't do anything for Beck.

I told Stevvie goodnight and walked back with him up the stairs. He climbed in bed, and I pulled the covers up and folded them under his arm to tuck him in. I set my hand on his forehead and moved some hair away from his face. I wished him sweet dreams and stood up to leave him.

"Jelli, will Beck be okay?" he asked, already with sleep swimming around in his voice.

I paused before closing the door.

"*I* think so. Now, get some sleep, kiddo."

I stood in the kitchen for a while, feeling antsy, feeling like I was forgetting something important. But I knew I hadn't forgotten anything. I looked to the wall where there was still the faintest stain of blue from the jar Beck had broken when Stevvie first came here. I wanted that version of Beck back. I would rather have a sad, angry and violent Beck than one who would take pleasure in seeing me dead.

And now, I had *no* version of him. All I had was a memory of our last encounter to haunt me, my waking nightmare.

I forced myself to breathe, when I zoned back in and realized I hadn't. I walked to the bedroom, closing the door with both hands, trying to make myself close it quietly in spite of my wanting to slam it and break the screaming silence around me. I leaned my forehead against the door and sighed quickly before pulling myself back up and making my way around the bed.

I pulled the bedding back to get in, but my legs wouldn't bend so I could get on the bed. I put the covers back and smoothed out the wrinkles with my palm. I turned my back to the bed and my legs gave out entirely, so suddenly I was kneeling on the carpet. The blueberry keychain was on the nightstand to my right, and I reached up and brought it to my other hand.

I stared at it and started crying. The world tilted and my arm was hit fairly hard. I lay on my side with tears rolling sideways along my freckled face. I pulled my legs closer to my torso. My tears made a small wet spot on the carpet against my cheek. This somehow made it scratchier, and I wanted to move, but more than that, I wanted to shrink until I collapsed in on myself.

I didn't do either of those things. I simply laid there, becoming as dehydrated as I was exhausted, crying inaudibly until sleep became me.

I woke up when it was still very dark outside.

I had felt a hand on my face, heavy and cold, bending my skin with the force of its touch, but when I rubbed away my dried tears, I saw that I was entirely alone. I sat up feeling uneasy, not from the but by something else.

I leaned back against the bed and looked out the window. There wasn't anything to see - it was much too dark - yet I continued to watch.

My face was wet again from tears I hadn't realized I still had in me. I wiped my cheeks and eyes with the front of my shirt and stood up. *I can't just sit here.* I walked around the house until my legs started to feel sore, and with that I went to sit on the porch. The lights were making a whining noise, and the summer night air was surprisingly cold. It was wonderfully comforting.

Pulling the collar of my shirt up to keep bugs from bothering me as much, I leaned against the supporting post and drifted again into slumber.

Stevvie sat next to me and carefully set a bowl on my lap to wake me. He had gotten us both cereal. I pulled my shirt off of my mouth to be able to eat, thanked him and quenched the hunger. In between spoonsful of his own, he threw an old ball for Marie. She ran and barked on the way to get it while he chewed. She returned, and they repeated the process.

When I finished the cereal, I drank the milk and licked my lips, looking up to see if I had to turn off the lights, but Stevvie had already done it.

"Hey kid, would you like to help me harvest more of the garden today? If there's anything that's ready?"

"Yeah!" he said, throwing the ball as hard and far as he could.

Visitor

We were working in the garden. There turned out to be a lot more work to do than I originally anticipated. There were a lot of crops ready, but the bigger job was the weeds that had been growing. *We really should have been more vigilant on the up keep to this point.*

After a few hours of working I sat down, out of breath and overheating.

"Hey, how about we take a break for a little while, get some water and rest?"

"I'm okay. But you can if you want to." Stevvie was unfazed by the work. Stevvie looked up at me not long after saying that, probably due to my silence. The look on my face must have said it all and he added, "I guess I could use a drink."

I nodded with a light chuckle.

We sat in the kitchen drinking mix-in lemonade.

"I'm gonna move the car further from the house, just in case someone from The Camp comes to find us and sees it. It might take some time. Could you feed Marie something while I'm gone?"

The features of his face lowered just a little.

"Yep."

"Thanks, man." I lowered my face to his when he looked down at my mention of The Camp. I wanted to meet his eye to convey the sincerity of my gratitude for the small gesture. I knew he could handle his own without me here: he did survive six years almost entirely alone.

I finished my glass and left to move the car.

When I was about to swing my second leg into the car, I saw someone walking toward the house. *Who could that be?* I got back out and pulled the knife out of my pocket. They approached fairly quickly but they were still on foot so it took a while - enough time for me to make a plan for whatever may happen. I met them halfway.

He came directly to me, his face had no mark and their body language was pleasant at least on a surface level. I saw some familiarity in his face, but I couldn't quite tell how I might know him. I just assumed I had seen him in passing at The Camp.

"My name is Dave." He said when he was close enough.

"Hello, Dave. What do you want?" I said shortly. I didn't have time for whatever this could be and I really didn't want Stevvie to hear this guy and come out here.

His demeanor changed. His face lost its introductory kindness and his eyes sharpened beneath their brows.

"The boy. The doctor wants him."

"Not gonna happen." My voice was dull, and I took a deeper breath to square out my shoulders. He took a step forward.

"Now, see, that just isn't going to work." Another step, now he was getting too close for comfort. "I'm here for the little brat." He moved his hand to show a knife loosely in his grip. "Are we clear?"

"Yep." I took a smooth step forward, grabbing the hand he held the knife in and using my own, forcing it into his throat and dragging it through his flesh. He started choking and gagging on his own blood. It rolled from his mouth in a combination of spit and incomprehensible words.

He started to fall, so I helped him to his knees. I looked him in the eyes, which were wide with surprise and his clear fear of dying.

"Crystal clear. *Dave.*" I moved over and opened the door of the car, got behind him and used my weight to help pull him up and into the car.

I picked up his knife and slid it in the belt loop of my pants before getting into the car myself. I looked behind me at nothing in particular, his eyes were still wide, but they had lost their focus. I reached back and closed them.

"I'm sorry," I whispered as I turned to the windshield. I started up the car and began the journey to dispose of his body. "But nobody comes after my kid."

I left him in the car and walked in the direction I had driven from when the car would no longer drive. It took me longer than I had hoped to walk back home, and I wanted so badly to wash the blood from my hands. It made my skin itch and crawl as it dried.

I could hear Stevvie and the dog playing in the garden, giving me the perfect opportunity to sneak into the house unseen. I scrubbed the dried blood from my hands so aggressively that for a moment there, I could have sworn it was *my* hands which were the source of the blood. Eventually they were cleaned, on every surface, of my actions.

The same was done to the gravel and dirt up at the front of the house. I washed it down with the hose and turned over the surface levels with the bottom of my shoe. Soon there was no sign that the man had even existed. *Goodbye, Dave.* I shut off the water, headed into the house through to the back to meet up with Stevvie.

I leaned out the back door, holding onto the frame to keep from falling over.

"Stevvie, Marie, it's getting late. Come on inside," I hollered out to them. Marie shot out of the green, running from the opening in the fence to come to me. Stevvie took a moment longer and was covered in dirt and mud when he did appear.

He smiled widely at me as he passed to enter the house. "Have fun?" I asked, turning on the lights. We had some time before I really needed to, but I would rather have them on too early than too late.

"Yep! 'Till I fell over... but yeah, I had fun."

"How about this? I'll start the bath for you, and while you get cleaned up I'll make something to eat?" I asked, making my way to the basement.

"Yes please! I am *starved*!" he shouted at me, dramatically flinging himself into one of the chairs in the kitchen. I laughed and continued to walk away.

He came through the spare room with his hair a curly damp mess. If he were a cartoon character, he would have floated into the room on a wave of smell. He kept breathing in through his nose like he couldn't find enough air in the room and must search for more. I had made a sort of roast or stew; I always forgot what differentiates the two.

Stevvie melted into his chair and started slurping up his dinner loudly. He paused only to ask me a question.

"Why was there blood on the ground up front?"

I choked while trying to swallow, and dropped the hope that he hadn't noticed.

"Oh, yeah, I saw that too." I shrugged as realistically as I could manage. "I think that a bunny might have been caught by something bigger. I cleaned it up though, so there isn't a need to worry."

"Okay..." We both lowered our heads closer to the food to continue eating, but we happened to glance up to each other at the same time. He didn't seem to believe me. Something was off in the look of his face, and it wasn't from the steam rising from his bowl.

"Good?" I asked him, lifting my spoon. He nodded. His face softened, and he put the entirety of his attention back to the food in front of him.

He finished eating and went to bed, saying he was exhausted from running around all day. The dog licked his bowl clean - which he had set down for her - and followed him. This left me alone again with my thoughts. My hand shook enough for the liquid to run off and away from the other ingredients on my spoon. I hated taking lives, no matter the reason - I wasn't meant for it.

As it became darker, the moment of taking that life haunted me all the more. I spent the night hallucinating, seeing his blood on my hands, but this time it wouldn't wash off. Still, I tried, I burned through half of a bar of soap washing my hands again and again. They went from normal to raisin-like and then to blistered. Only after the blisters split and my hands began to bleed did I find myself able to turn off the water.

I fell back against the wall, realizing after I had that it was the same wall Stevvie was sleeping against. I held my breath and waited to see if the noise had woken him. It hadn't, and only then did I exhale. The water and blood dripped down to the ground between my legs. I watched the drops and focused on the sting of the air in the open wounds.

My arms rested on my upright legs and that gave me a clear view of what I had just done. I would wrap them in the morning, but for now I would simply look and wait for it to make up for the horrible things I had done earlier in the day, knowing full well that it never could. That man was *dead* because of me.

The night passed in a blur. I couldn't tell if I had slept or if I had just sat there staring at my hands for so long that I forgot to register that I wasn't dreaming.

When the sun was up, I turned off the lights and wrapped my hands. I made breakfast and waited for Stevvie to wake up. He asked about the bandages, to which I told him I had just burnt my hands making breakfast. I didn't like lying to him, but there I went, time and time again, lying poorly through my teeth.

He probably knew that I was lying now, just as he had over dinner the night before. But I had to tell myself that this dishonesty was what was best for the both of us. I had to tell myself that, because I wasn't sure if it was what was best, but I needed to feel some certainty, any certainty at all.

My hands hurt. The blisters bled and leaked, and every movement pulled at the gauze covering them. Stevvie was clearly eyeing the spots of bloody fluid pooling visibly after the first few clear times of me wincing. He set down his silverware.

"You can keep pretending, or you can tell me what's really going on."

I sighed. Debating. Several long moments of thought passed between us. In the end, I knew for a fact that this kid could handle whatever gets thrown his way.

"De sent someone from The Camp to get you. They would have used any force necessary to get you. Any -"

"If I went, it could save Beck...?" His face was serious and there was something burning in his eyes at the question he asked.

"It's not worth it. It's not worth your life. How do you live with the lives you have taken...?" I looked at him with tears in my eyes and asked.

He exhaled heavily.

"It's the only life I know. You didn't have to do anything like that before the Finish, did you?" I shook my head and mouthed the word 'never'. Stevvie nodded. "So they didn't make it?" I shook my head again. "And your hands?"

I lifted my hands up.

"I tried to wash away the guilt," I whispered. He seemed to understand.

Stevvie reached across the table and took my hand in his. This contact hurt, but the comfort it brought was worth the pain.

"It's okay." He smiled a small but genuine smile, and his voice had a steadiness to it that made me somehow so very sure that he was right. *It's okay.*

It hurt to do so, but I squeezed his hand in mine and mustered up the strength to nod.

We spent the day in the garden like we had the day before, though I couldn't do nearly the same amount of work with my hands in the condition they were in. This time, when we left, the garden looked almost like something out of a magazine.

How much has changed over these last seven years? How much have I changed? I have murdered... I have had to learn skills I never would have thought to know before the Finish. Have I changed as much as the rest of the world? I would have asked Stevvie these questions rather than just thinking them to myself, but I knew his answer would fall to something similar, but not identical to - 'I don't know, I never knew you before. Just like I never knew the world before.' Either way, it wasn't his job to answer my existential questions.

I didn't know what to do with myself. The house felt wrong, like that which belonged to a stranger, without Beck here. That feeling stayed and grew with each passing day. It got to the point that Stevvie tried to intervene. He brought me downstairs to the basement and handed me a stick of chalk.

"What's this for?" I asked him, holding it up.

"For drawing." He insisted, really quite smiley.

I sighed.

"I know that... I'm asking why you handed it to me?"

"For drawing. You seem sad..." He gestured to the ground. "Draw your feelings out?"

I thought about it for a moment before making my way to the floor. The floor was still a little wet from when he had washed his other drawing away to make room for mine. He patted me on the top of the head, like I would have done to him, before leaving me alone in an empty room intended to be decorated by the things I couldn't describe. *Perhaps it will make sense in color?*

Fittingly, the chalk which Stevvie had handed me was blue. I drew random lines and tried my best to chase away this emptiness, one colorful stroke at a time. I went through a good third of that stick before becoming frustrated at something, perhaps myself, and picking up the red.

This rollercoaster continued on, color after color, emotion after emotion, until I found myself waking up to a small hand cupping my shoulder. I must have become too exhausted and fallen asleep while scribbling, I still had the chalk in my hand.

"It's beautiful," he said, very matter-of-factly in his high, youthful voice. *It's shit at best,* I thought to myself, but I decided it better to not speak my response. Instead, I simply thanked him.

"How late is it?" I changed the subject.

"Morning. You must have been very tired after drawing all this." His hands spread and his eyes widened, looking around the floor behind me. I turned to see so much more of the ground drawn on than I thought I had done. It still looked like shit to me, but a kind of poetic disaster, a visual aid to the unraveling of an individual.

"Oh," I breathed out.

"Hey, um, I'm hungry but I can't reach the cereal I want. Will you help me?" he asked like a kid asking to stay up past their bedtime.

"Of course." I jumped to my feet and went up the steps with him and to the kitchen. I grabbed his cereal for him. I washed the chalk from my hands before mixing the milk for the kid's breakfast. He hopped into the chair excitedly and ate like he knew it was his last meal.

I felt a little hungry myself, it felt as if some of the numbness had subsided, so I decided to join Stevvie. *Did his whole 'draw out your feelings' idea work?* I didn't expect it to, but I guess a small piece of me had hoped it would.

The cereal tasted astonishingly similar to cardboard, but I was blissfully happy that it had a taste at all. By the looks of it, Stevvie felt the same. Once-powdered milk dribbled down his little face, but he didn't seem to notice as he was too busy repeatedly stuffing more of the stale, bland cereal into his mouth.

The next few days were a bit better, but still they dragged on painfully.

I tried to keep from making Stevvie miserable too, but against my efforts it did wear off on him. Clearly it did. He started spending less and less time around me, which wasn't difficult to do because I hardly left Beck's room, but even with meals and things like that he seemed obviously and intentionally avoidant.

Independent Decisions

It was probably the second or third day I had spent in Beck's room, without leaving, when Stevvie finally came in to check on me. He sat on the ground next to me and joined me in my staring at the carpet. He set his hand on my knee. Even with him joining me, I felt all alone without Beck in this room.

"I want to go to The Camp." he said so quietly that for a moment I thought I had imagined it.

"What?" I looked up at him in a daze.

"I want to save Beck."

I heard him clearly this time.

"No. It's too dangerous. The risks are too high! We don't even know what De will do to you."

"I want to do whatever it takes to save him. The dark got him, and he changed. He changed like my mom did... I don't want him to die like her, too..." He was clearly fighting back tears, blinking hard to keep them at bay. I grabbed his hand.

"He has De's cure; he won't die."

"But he won't be himself..." He was quiet again.

That sentence tore its way through my chest. I swallowed hard, trying to find the words to ask what Stevvie meant, but I knew what he meant. *It would be a less cruel fate for him to die than to live trapped in pieces inside himself, rotting away slowly.* I squeezed his hand and asked him a question when my throat could finally muster the strength to speak.

"Are you *sure* that this is what you want?"

He nodded and pulled his hand from mine before walking from the room.

I guess we would be going to The Camp after all.

Day One

    We waited until the next morning, and with the sun, the three of us left, packed and trying to be ready for whatever chaos may await us at our destination.

    It was a particularly hot day. They seemed to rise in temperature with the passing of each one. We kept our skin covered in light layers and tried to stay hydrated. The ground was dry and hard under our heavy feet. By the time we could see Namma's house the scar on my foot felt like a fresh wound again.

    Stevvie knocked, because at that point I was carrying the majority of the bags. Namma was wonderfully happy to see us: at first, that is. She looked for Beck, and when she didn't find him standing among us, her smile dropped to something weak and fake. She stepped to the side and welcomed us in.

"So, where is he now? Off wandering some other place he doesn't need to?" she asked, thinking he had just disappeared again. "Did he leave another note at least?"

"De has him."

Her sarcasm stopped, and her head snapped to me.

"That boy isn't d—" She couldn't finish the rest of the sentence, so I stepped in and answered it anyway.

"No, he's alive, but he's infected. Second stage." The words fell numbly from my lips.

"So he *is* dead." She cared about him like he was her own child. This was present in how hard it was for her to keep her sadness at bay.

"No." I said. She looked confused and a little hurt when I said this, thinking I was pulling her leg or playing some joke, but I wasn't. "De made a cure. It doesn't fix anything, but it does stop it from progressing any further."

"That crazy bastard did it?" she asked. It seemed as if she was talking to the floor. She thought to herself for a moment before speaking again to me. "Are there any side effects?"

"I'm not sure... De didn't say anything."

She mumbled under her breath, something like 'of course he didn't,' and I continued.

"But knowing what we know about the infected and the stages... some brain damage could be expected. The extent, however... completely subjective."

She grabbed the lower half of her face in her right hand and began to slowly pace. Both Stevvie and I followed her steps as she moved. She stopped, but not before I was dizzy, and she looked at us and spoke.

"Hungry?" Namma asked. She disappeared into the kitchen before we could even answer.

Stevvie dragged our things to some cots and sat on the floor to work on math with cards. Marie seemed to be taped to his leg. She hardly ever left his side these days.

I decided to wait in the doorway and watch Namma cook. I would have offered to help, but I knew better: When she gets all 'thinky' before she cooks, it's best to just stay out of her way. You *can* help her, but only if you aren't particularly fond of all of your fingers. Such a strongly willed woman as she can become dangerous when she is battling her thoughts, and I learned to steer clear.

Either way, she might not have even noticed me, she was deeply lost in her thoughts. I was sure enough that the only other thing that could catch her attention was the food she was making. So I just watched her think as she moved about the space.

The air went from a bland, dusty stench of emptiness to smelling gloriously of crust and meat and vegetables. Namma cleaned as the food - which I gathered was some kind of meat pie - cooked in the wood oven, building upon the smell as it did.

She kept tidying up, even after the room was more than clean. *Many things to think over, I guess.* After she washed the same dish for what must have been the sixth time, I had to intervene, even if it cost me a finger or two. I went up to her and pulled her hands out of the sink and held them in mine.

"It'll be okay." I bowed and lowered my head to her eyeline to get her to focus on me. "We have a way to fix it... We might be able to really cure him," I whispered to her. Her eyes widened and clung to mine.

"What?"

I glanced at the back room where I knew the boy was playing. "Stevvie. He's immune."

"Immu—" I interrupted her with a nod.

"That's why we're going back to The Camp, so Stevvie can help De to come up with a genuine solution."

"No!" Suddenly she was very urgent and grabbed my arms to pull me closer. "He will *kill* that little boy." she whispered harshly, she was trying to be quiet so Stevvie wouldn't hear, but she wasn't quiet, not by a long shot.

"I know. He knows. It's his choice. All I can do is try to keep him safe as best as I can."

"You can't!" Her voice grew louder.

"It's not my choice." I said as clearly as I could.

Silence hung around us for a moment.

"I hope his decision is worth it, and I hope your attempts to keep him safe aren't in vain." She said it earnestly and smiled to push the point further. She then pulled away to take the food out of the oven. "It needs to cool down for a bit before it can be eaten. In the meantime, I will be back. I need to freshen up." She touched a spot of flour on her wrinkled and sun-spotted cheek before walking away.

"And I thought the food *you* made was good!" Stevvie said through a mouthful of Namma's food. I would have been hurt by such a clear- though unintentional- insult, but I couldn't help but agree with him. I nodded while taking another bite. Namma laughed at this little interaction, shrugging lightly and making a funny face at me.

Although we tried very hard to keep the air about us light, we all had heavy realities weighing down on our minds.

We finished eating and stumbled away to our beds before falling heavily to sleep.

Day Two

We slept well at Namma's house. It felt so sweet and welcoming to us, rather than the suffocating and crushing feeling that came with Beck's house. We waved goodbye to her front door, but we didn't say it to her. She was still asleep when we left, so we decided it best to just let her rest.

Today was hot as well, but with nourishing food in our systems to push us forward, the scorching heat seemed much less like being in a pan on hot and drowning in butter. Still, we hid our skin from the sky's fire.

We walked with more gusto in our steps, which gave us a speed we hadn't seen in a while. This was quite nice: it meant we were putting more distance behind us and giving ourselves more time to rest throughout our journey, and more water breaks to combat the heat and physical excursion. Marie seemed to appreciate these the most with her coat of fur.

About halfway through the day I decided we should take an exceptionally long break. I used the excuse that we were 'making such great time,' when in reality it was that each step closer to The Camp made me want to vomit. We may very likely be marching to put Stevvie to death. Similar to being forced from The Camp, yet worse, we were *choosing* to be one of De's little experiments.

We stopped, planning just to sit and drink, but plans changed when a rabbit went jumping nearby.

"Hey." I leaned in near the boy and whispered. "Do you think you could shoot it in the head, leaving the rest intact?" I wanted his aim to be as good as I remembered it, just in case he might need it for De.

He didn't respond, he just looked at me, his eyes a bit doubting and his lower lip sticking out. The minute the gun was out from behind the large belt that he still insisted on wearing, the entire atmosphere around him changed. His face calmed and became serious. His hands were steady with the gun out in front of him. He took a short breath when the rabbit turned to face him and he fired.

It was as close to a perfect shot as I could have imagined, though it left my ears ringing violently. We went to get the rabbit and gut it before leaving to go to the next step. I strapped it to the back of my bag to let it bleed out a stream as I walked.

There was an ever-so-thinning trail of blood marking where we walked. I tried to figure out if we could time another stop for long enough to finish prepping and cook the rabbit or if it would have to wait and we would just end up trading it off at The Camp. We snacked on some stale crackers while we walked, it dried our mouths much more than it filled our stomachs.

I started playing this sort of game, like I used to do on my way to school as a kid. I kicked a rock again and again for as far as I could. When I would lose the rock I was kicking, like I kicked it too far out of my designated path, I would then pick the next half-decent rock I came across and continue the game. It was more entertaining than I had thought it would be and even more so than I remembered from my childhood. *I'm glad I get to have little moments with him, moments like this, I may not get the opportunity to give him more...*

Stevvie caught onto what I was doing on one of the times I kicked it far enough where I would have to obviously side-step to catch it with my dragging feet. He looked at me funny, but I tried to ignore it. He continued to watch me for a while. Not too long after catching his attention did I kick another rock in front of where he was walking.

I gave up on that rock and began to glance ahead to see if there were any really good contenders I could steer toward. Stevvie, on the other hand, had other ideas. He looked down, kicked the stone I had last, watched it as it toppled to where I could reach it and smiled while waiting for my reaction. I smiled back and nudged it lightly again, this time intentionally aiming to the ground ahead of him. We passed the same rock back and forth for a long time, and when we lost it, another would take its place.

We got lost in the game enough to not notice our walking but not enough to lose our direction. We came up to the house very quickly, which was a surprise to us both. Stevvie had the rock last, and he kicked it far to his right, away from the both of us, before running up to the door.

The sun was still a while from setting, too high to call it a sunset but low enough that it reddened the edges of the horizon. I turned the door handle, hot from the direct lighting, flung the door open and waved for Stevvie to enter first.

I camped down in the corner, right away, tired from walking and the worry that hung heavily in my head. There was still some wax melted into the hard flooring and I could still see the blackened spot of blood spilt by Beck so long ago. Stevvie chose a wall to sleep by, but first he practiced with his math cards, he was getting quite good with them. *I should get him some higher-level learning supplies; he's a smart kid, and he enjoys gaining knowledge. I think it'll be good for him.*

He would be in the first grade by now... It was strange to think about how young he would be in the world before this. And now... well, now he is choosing to risk his life to *try* to save other people.

He packed up his cards and laid out a sleeping bag, quickly falling asleep with Marie curled up by his side. The sun was only now setting, and with the sun, I, too, fell into a quiet, dark slumber. The last thing I could remember crossing my mind before sleeping was that I was glad the smell of my vomit was no longer present. Then, unlike the flashlights we had hung from the ceiling, all three of us were out.

We woke up before sunrise. It was nice; it was quiet. We waited a while for the sun to join us.

23

Day Three

We ate a small breakfast of some bland bread with a little blueberry jam slathered on top. Stevvie clearly thought it was delicious, he even almost took back the insult to my cooking - there was, after all, a reason I was named 'Jelli'. For the dog, I cut off some of the still-raw rabbit. When we were done eating, we could just barely see the edge of the sun pulling its way up from its rest within the folds of the horizon.

By the time we had repacked and were ready to leave, the sun was the one waiting for us.

Today we would be walking that last bit of distance to The Camp. How we felt about it was clear in our slow and complaint-filled pace. It was almost as if our bodies knew on a cellular level exactly what we were walking to and were trying strongly to prevent it, or at very least delay it. But even though it wasn't what we wanted, it was inevitable. It was what Stevvie wanted, and I was *going* to be there for him every step of the way.

We had been walking in silence for a long time, so when Stevvie spoke it honestly startled me.

"Thank you," he said.

I raised my gaze to find that he was looking at the scar on his right hand. "Thank you. Both you and Beck showed me a lot of kindness. You gave me a lot. And now, you are walking with me..." His voice trailed off, but I knew what he was saying.

I reached down and took his left hand tightly in my right. "Thank you..."

"For what?" he seemed genuinely confused.

"You gave us the one thing we wanted more than anything, but simply couldn't have." He was still staring at me confused, so I just smiled, tried to not cry and gently squeezed his hand before letting it go. He, however, didn't let go. He didn't know what I was talking about, but he held onto a few of my fingers in a way that said that although he didn't fully understand, he knew.

Our speed was pathetic; a dead man could have moved faster if he had any reason to, but we simply couldn't force ourselves to progress any faster. Honestly it seemed like we were digging our feet into the sand more with each step, simply so that it would slow us that much more.

I pulled my hand from Stevvie's to turn and throw up, having realized just how close we were to The Camp. It was a sickly blue and brown-gray color and smelled fairly sweet of the blueberries that also gave it such an appearance. He asked me what was wrong, but my response was simply throwing up again. My stomach was so knotted from the idea of leading that child into the hands that lacked morals, that it was physically painful. I glanced ahead, dizzily, and my stomach knotted again, tighter this time. It was difficult for me to fight off that third round of vomit.

"I'm fine," I lied blatantly after failing to hold back the puke in my throat, with it rolled out the pain in my gut which, too, left my lips. This had made Stevvie ask again if I was okay. "We should keep walking. We won't make it there today if we don't hurry." *I don't want to get stuck in the dark.* I knew we probably would, though. By the sun's position in the sky and the markers on the ground, I knew we would almost certainly have to spend the night in the dark. Especially if we didn't start walking faster, which I didn't see happening.

He clearly didn't believe the lie, and I couldn't make it more realistic, because puking had made me dizzy enough to where standing on my feet seemed to be a struggle all on its own. I swayed hard, and he put out his arms to catch me. He wouldn't have been able to, but as a reflex, it was sweet.

I started to walk again, even though the world spun around me.

"I don't believe you." His small voice was coming from behind me, but kind of sounded like it was coming from everywhere at once. I turned to look at him, and after my vision refocused, I saw that he was crying a little.

"Sit. Drink some water," he said. Even in his young voice it was a command that I didn't feel like fighting. Even the way Marie sat near him seemed like she was agreeing with him.

I made my way to the ground - it was more of falling than sitting - but I ended up on the ground, and that was good enough for me. I pulled out my water and sipped a little, making sure to watch him as I did so.

"We don't have time for this," I said, exhausted, and held back gagging.

"Yes, we do." The way he said it told me that he too had come to the conclusion that we would spend tonight in the dark.

Stevvie and Marie came to my side, she sniffed my throw up, and I nudged her to keep her from trying to eat it. Stevvie took my bags from me and pulled the little tent from where he had seen me pack it. He waved his hands at my attempts of advice or help and kept working away until the tent was up. He hung the lights but left them off, and tossed out sleeping bags on either side.

He motioned for me to go inside and had to tell the dog to stay with me. I did as he said, and then he left. Stevvie wasn't gone for too long, but when he came back he was carrying several rocks. He laid them out in a circle not far from the front of the tent. He disappeared again, this time to find some kindling.

He started up a fairly nice fire in no time at all.

I, now at the door, scooted over to give Stevvie room to sit by me and started cooking the rabbit over the fire. The three of us ate it and some canned beans, turning on the lights before laying down to bed.

I was facing the wall of the tent, honestly thinking that he had fallen asleep, but I spoke to him anyway.

"Are you a hundred percent sure you want to go to The Camp tomorrow?"

He whispered back to me.

"Yes. I can help Beck, so I will. It's the right thing to do." *The right thing to do... De enjoys telling me to do that, though I don't think it's something he knows anything about.* With that, the both of us fell asleep soundly.

24

Day Four

I spent the night in fear, even in sleep, of the darkness that lived around us.

Marie was the first of us to wake up, we quickly followed her lead when she started barking like her life depended on it. Stevvie and I shot up. He grabbed his gun, and I grabbed Beck's favorite knife, but when we looked outside, we saw that there was nothing but the wind. The both of us wanted to go back to sleep, but we knew better than to follow that urge. We began to pack up and prepare to leave.

The sun was still low in the sky, which was good for us because we were walking quite slowly again. Also luckily for us, we had walked more than half of the way the day before. Our feet seemed to be moving backwards, they wanted it so badly, but against what we felt and what we wished, we walked on forward.

Every time we stopped to rest, have some water, I had to fight the desire to run in the opposite direction as quickly as my legs would carry me. In support of the boy and his decision, I made myself sit still and try to just relax.

The day passed bit by bit and eventually, on the fine line of the horizon, we could see the concrete walls of the seventy second camp of the North American region. A new level of strength to Stevvie's steps as we saw it and suddenly he was walking with courage in his strides, I however felt more defeated.

The walls of The Camp loomed over us but we kept our heads high. And as we got closer, I knew the guards were watching us. I didn't look; I could just feel it in the skin of my neck. I wouldn't give them the satisfaction of being looked up at. No, I held my chin up and my eyes steadily forward.

We stepped through the gates. *No turning back now.*

25

Sweat trickled from my hairline and down my spine, sending chills through the skin of my back as we walked by the houses. I tried to blame the heat, but what an obvious lie that was. My hands were shaking, though I thought it was only in my head. Stevvie took my hand to steady it as we walked. *How was he so calm? I wasn't the one in danger. The worst that would happen to me is some scolding from De, but Stevvie...*

We came to the house at the back wall, the entrance to the stairs, where he tightened his grip on my hand. I looked at his face, but still he seemed okay. The gesture was more so for me than for him.

Walking down those steps felt like watching a horror movie. No matter how much I would scream for the people to not go down them, they wouldn't hear me, and they would keep walking. I would keep walking, in spite of the screaming voice in my head.

I grabbed Stevvie's arm hard and he turned to face me.

"We can go." He closed his eyes and shook his head. His little hand raised up and rested on mine, I softened my grip and we continued walking.

Down the corridor and the second staircase we went.

De didn't notice us at first. He didn't notice us until I cleared my throat loudly, and with that, he turned to us, surprised.

"Well, look who we have here..."

Stevvie began to step forward. I hadn't let go of his hand, and I pulled him to a halt. He looked up at me confused, down to his hand and then back to me. His eyes said loudly 'let me go, let me do this,' so I did.

Stevvie walked to the doctor proudly.

"I want to make a cure. I want to help Beck." Stevvie said. Beck's head shot up when the kid spoke his name and De looked over to me. Beck turned to me and smiled, I wanted to throw up again but put a hand over my mouth to help keep it down.

"Are you sure?" De didn't break eye contact with me as he asked Stevvie this question. It almost seemed like he was asking me. Even Stevvie looked at me before answering.

"Yes. I'm sure." He stared De down, forcing him to look away from me.

"Good." The doctor turned back to his desk, pulling out a chair for Stevvie and patted it. He started shuffling around in one of the desks. "Sit." He pointed a gloved hand to the seat, and Stevvie listened to him.

De picked up one of the jars from the desk, moved Stevvie's hand palm-up, upended the jar, and filled his hand with the blackened blood of the infected. Stevvie flinched, but the old man grabbed him and forced him to be still.

"Good. Good," he mumbled, turning around and digging through the desk again. "Pour that back in the jar as best you can boy." He held the jar behind him for the boy to grab. He did, and followed the doctor's directions again.

"Tell me, why are you still here?" He turned to me before bending back down to Stevvie, who looked at me with pleading eyes.

"I'm not leaving again. I'm gonna do what's best for Stevvie." I mentally screamed at my legs to move and was surprised when they listened. I walked to them. I gently grabbed the boy's shoulder and stood strong, staring at De, who wouldn't look up at me.

"Are you *certain* that is what is *best*?" He put an IV into Stevvie's arm, causing him to wince.

I took Stevvie's hand in mine and gave him a look that said it would all be okay. He smiled slightly at me and went back to watching De work, his smile vanishing.

"Yes. I *am* certain," I said.

De took several small vials of Stevvie's blood and labeled them, setting all but one away in his desk. He played with that separated vial, passing it between his hands and studying the liquid as it ran around its small glass cage. He took out Stevvie's IV and put a bandaid in its place to stop the blood.

"Go on, now." He glanced between the both of us before turning away to keep watching the vial and setting his hand on the back of the chair. "But stay close. I'll call for you when I need you." He spoke sternly and quickly flipped the chair around and under his own legs just as soon as Stevvie was out of it.

"Yes, Sir." I mumbled sarcastically under my breath as Stevvie and I walked rapidly away from him, almost running for the sanctuary that those steps represented. We got to the top of them, entirely out of his sight, running through the other corridor and the other set of stairs. When we were back outside, we both stopped to catch our breath. Stevvie began to sway some, I pulled him into a side hug to help and keep him up on his feet.

"Let's get you something to eat and drink." I put my arm under his and we made our way to the front of The Camp.

"We should also get checked in." His voice sounded so much more like that of a child now that he was tired.

It was dark, and with both the weight of the bags and Stevvie being exhausted and having given blood, we walked slowly. I didn't mind it too much though. It was almost nice, like a lamplit stroll after the journey we pushed through in the past few days.

We got checked in, but they weren't offering anything at the cafeteria, so we just went to the house they had assigned us. Once there, I dug to the bottom of my bag and found a drink mix-in. It was well expired, but it was better than nothing. I shook it into my water and handed it to Stevvie, who started sipping away at it.

Marie, who we told to wait outside of De's 'lair,' wouldn't leave Stevvie's side from the moment we got out. She cuddled up with him, and they both fell asleep. I tried to sleep as well, but I was having a very hard time. *Stevvie was strong, like always, stronger than I tend to give him credit for.* But what kept me awake was how still and quiet

Beck had been while we were down there, simply watching us.

I rolled over and shoved my face into the pillow. This made breathing a little more difficult, but for once I needed to sleep without the lights in my eyes. After doing so, it wasn't long before I was resting peacefully. I had a dream - more like a memory - of Beck, Sammy and myself on a foraging trip.

It was just as I remembered it.

It was the first foraging trip we went on after giving her the blueberry keychain. We said that she could go on her own, but she insisted on us coming along with her. She understood that although she was resourceful enough to travel alone, in this world, it was almost always safer to travel in groups.

Per her pleas, Beck and I went along. It was fun, though. We all enjoyed our time together, out in the world, rather than watching it from the safety of lights and windows and locks.

The trip couldn't have taken more than a week, one or two days to leave, a few to scavenge and just over three days to walk back. We hadn't found anything majorly notable, just common findings, which we added to our small stash of resources anyway.

In the Finish, everything had some value. This constant drive for survival and self-preservation forced onto people a kind of hoarder's mentality. With items you never before would have thought to be important, you now might be willing to risk getting caught in the dark just to chance having it.

It's interesting to see how people change to adapt to their surroundings and how others know nothing but this frame of mind.

I woke up with a smile on my face, but as the memory faded back into being nothing more than a memory so too did the smile fade from my face. *We are just waiting for De to call.* The reality of it made me want to puke until there was nothing much left but stomach acid, like I had two days before. *Feels like an eternity.*

I stretched and listened to the choir of cracks my tired body made, I yawned and then even my ears popped. My head felt heavy and leaned for the pillow with some fight to it, but I didn't lay back down. I stood to stop the feeling.

I stood there for a while, doing nothing really, not even thinking, just blankly trying both to sleep again and to keep from sleeping. Eventually Marie woke Stevvie up because she had to go outside and use the bathroom. So, tiredly rubbing his eyes, he got up and let her out. When he came back in, with more day in him, he smiled at me and spoke. "Good morning."

I blinked rapidly and pulled myself out of my daze. "Good morning." I tried to return the smile, but it felt weird on my face, and I assumed it looked strange as well, not that Stevvie's expression showed anything to back that. "Breakfast?" I asked him although I still felt a bit like puking out my guts.

"Yes please!" He ushered Marie into the house and the both of us traded places with her. "I'll bring you back something tasty, okay?" He whispered to the dog before closing the door, but she whimpered in spite of his promise.

Stevvie carried himself much easier as we walked to the school cafeteria. He still looked weaker than his normally perky self, but he did look much better than he had the night before. I guess the traveling and the horrible sleep and nutrition combined with De being his 'charming' self, just took too much out of him and something had to give. Hopefully some food will have the same effects as last night's sleep had.

It did.

Stevvie ate so much that he began to look a little green, like he was fighting to keep it all down. He snuck some food into his pocket after very obviously looking around to make sure no one was watching him. He nodded to me as a way of saying 'mission completed, we can go now.' I laughed lightly and nodded back to him.

Stevvie was on his feet before I could grab the apple on my plate. He ran around the table and started pulling on my shirt sleeve. I stood up so he wouldn't pull me to my ass, and we walked back to the house. You would think that being out in the daylight would be less unnerving than its darker counterpart, but it wasn't. Every person who came too close we thought was sent by De. We were both on our toes.

Marie greeted Stevvie like he had been gone for a century. He pulled the food from his pocket for her and sat by her side while she ate. He ran his hand over the top of her head as she scarfed down the few miscellaneous consumable items.

"Good girl, Marie. Good girl." He spoke softly to her. Something in that moment told me that if he got the chance to grow up, this world wouldn't be able to harden him completely. Stevvie would always have kind eyes and a heart that was kinder still.

We heard a knock not long after coming back from breakfast. Both Stevie and I froze in place at the sound and watched the door, waiting for it to burst off of its hinges. A moment long pause, and then a second knock, this time quieter, weaker. I walked to answer it. I didn't feel like Stevvie should have to be the one to do it.

"We heard you guys were back here. Can Stevvie play?" It was two children, not someone sent at the hands of De, as we had expected. The children had a noticeable resemblance to each other. One was clearly older though; perhaps they were siblings. The older one was standing back with a hand on the younger one's shoulder, and the smaller child was cradling one of their hands in the other, like it was hurt.

"I'm sorry. I am really busy." Stevvie said, stepping around me. "Maybe some other day?" The children nodded and said 'okay' not seeming too upset by the rejection, and sauntered off, most likely to find some other children to play with. With that Stevvie closed the door. I looked at him, but before I could ask why - even though I almost certainly knew why - he told me. "I need to save my energy. De might call."

"Then I guess we relax?" I said, not entirely sure what that last word meant, not at this moment, at least. We both walked aimlessly around the front area of the house for a while, before realizing the pointlessness of it and sitting down to read and fill the silence with thoughts of other people's words.

I pulled out a thin book, one I always carried with me but never read and almost never seemed to remember. It was a book about law, the fourth of eleven just like it. It reminded me of the world I came from, but it kept me from having to lug around books almost as heavy as me. It was worn from years of use long before being lost in my backpack for 'safe' keeping. The words to most would be mind-numbing, but to me they described the fascinating structure of the world of rules and justice.

Stevvie pulled out a book as well, but I was much too lost in the well-read and deeply familiar words that I didn't take note of what it was he was reading. He too, as far as I could tell, was enjoyably lost in the pages of whatever children's book he was practicing his reading with.

He whispered the words to himself. Though I didn't pay any attention to what he was saying, he was saying it with serious focus and attention to detail. I had noticed before that it was always a little bit easier for him to read if he spoke, even just at a whisper, or at very least mouthed the words.

I got so lost in the familiarity of the text and the memories it brought back to me, that when I heard a knocking sound interrupting my reading, I looked up half expecting to see Jay. Then reality came flooding back in... Stevvie, De, all of it. I stiffened and shoved the book back into my bag where I knew it would be forgotten and neglected for a very long time once again.

Stevvie was the first to the door.

"The doctor wants you. Says you know where to find him." This stranger's nasally voice made the back of my eyes hurt. It was so annoying, and her unplaceable accent didn't help the matter much either. She turned and walked off, and as she was walking away, she said one last thing. "And you'd better hurry. He seemed pissed off."

"Shit." I exhaled the cuss and patted the dog on the head before walking out of the house with the kid.

"You know you don't have to come with me." Stevvie said. He seemed nervous and kept wringing his hands.

"I'm not going to leave you alone in this. I'm not going to leave you with *him*." I smiled, and I could tell that this eased his nerves a little. He reached up and took my hand.

"Thank you, Jelli."

26

Almost Twelve Years Later

I woke up with a start. It was probably just a mouse getting caught in a trap somewhere out of my sight; they were an especially large problem this year. I think it was just how horrible this winter was, forcing all of the mice out of their shitty shelters in the rubble, out of what was once a world and into The Camp.

This last winter was arguably worse than the first one that the Finish had seen, only this time, we were prepared. The cold was colder, but we had food, and we had numbers. Most importantly, we had some small sliver of hope to give us the strength to fight. We did fight, through months and months, but God was the relief almost audible when the cold finally did show signs of breaking.

I yawned, my body interrupting itself with a shiver. The weather was warming, but it still wasn't a day in paradise. Something was caught in my field of vision: it was stuck to my forehead, and I pulled it off. *Paper.* I sighed. *I fell asleep at the desk again.* Gently, I place the small paper back where it belonged in the chaos in front of me.

I tried to pop my back against the chair, but it simply crunched and stiffened more. *I'm too young to have a back this old.* A disturbingly twisted - but now so very familiar - voice drifted toward me from the wall of nearly empty cages at my back.

"Morning?"

He was just taunting my efforts.

"Shut the fuck up," I mumbled. I wasn't in the mood today to deal with this. Most of the day had already been wasted by sleep; I wouldn't let him waste any more of it. I was at the bottom of the stairs when I turned to Beck. "No, it's afternoon," I taunted him in his confinement, and his hands tightened around the bars. His dark eyes followed me up the steps until I was no longer in his view.

Not a minute later, I was standing in the mid-afternoon light. The sun on my skin was so much warmer than the irritating bulbs which I spent most of my time beneath these days. It felt nice to be in the sun. I could have stayed there until my bones turned to dust and drifted off into the wind, but my stomach kept protesting, growling and groaning away at me.

"Fine." I whispered downward. "I'll eat something." I rolled my eyes, mostly at myself, I honestly couldn't remember the last time I had eaten anything at all. I made my way through the camp to the school. My legs hurt, but walking on them felt wonderful even with the pain.

I grabbed some food, it looked like soup, but it could have been anything if made poorly enough. I sat down at one of the cafeteria tables and ate the mysterious soup. It tasted like dishwater and had a texture similar to what you would pull out of a garbage disposal, but it was edible enough and more than welcome.

I left, not feeling much better. My stomach was still grumbling. This time, however, I could tell it was more of a 'what the fuck was *that*' kind of disturbance. The sun took away my attention again; it was bright and warm, and when I closed my eyes, I could see the blue veins in my eyelids contrasting against the pink-ish hues of the skin.

I heard someone call my name and I opened my eyes, I smiled at them and nodded as they walked by. I couldn't quite see who it was - there were sunspots blotting out my vision.

I stayed out and walked around The Camp, just enjoying the outdoors as much as I could before I disappeared back into the wall for who knows how long, again. I greeted the people of The Camp, checking up on a few here and there. But after a few short hours of this, I knew I couldn't prolong the inevitable any longer. Although my body wanted to be out here, my mind needed to be there, inches from a breakthrough. *Now I can almost see why De was crazy...*

I went down those two flights of stairs and back to the desk.

"Miss me already?" Beck said as I walked past him to sit in the chair. I just ignored him, I had too much to think about to let him start saying shit to get in my head. I scooted the chair closer to the table, which I often referred to as a 'desk' De had put drawers and cabinets on and all around it enough to constitute it as a desk, and began to reread my most recent notes.

I pulled out a new vial and began to make changes based on a combination of information De had left me and the information I had been gathering myself. So I worked, time blurred, Beck's foul and ever growing violent speeches drifted away, and my thoughts filled with everything in front of me and nothing else.

It must have been night at least by the time that a sense of time came back to me. My ass hurt from sitting still and I realized that I desperately needed to pee. I got up and stretched. Beck must have gotten tired of trying to verbally lacerate me and had fallen asleep, because the room was silent. I broke the noise, moving the chair out of my way and back to its home tucked under the table.

I went through the motions of climbing the steps, staying in the house which fronted for the entrance to the 'lair' to relieve myself before going outside. I was right, at least partly; it was night, but the horizon was a bit light and yellowed. At first I thought it was that the sun was setting, but I knew it was the wrong side of the sky for that to be the truth. *I worked all night, again.*

Suddenly, I felt that much more tired. My body ached, my head was pounding, and my eyes began to fight to close: they were simply too heavy to hold themselves up any longer. I craved rest, and for the first time in a long time, I craved it - craved something - more than finding answers. *Okay... Okay.* I thought, losing a fight with myself. *I will sleep.*

I went through the streets, under the safety of the bright lights, all of the way back to the house. It had seemed like years since I had last stepped foot inside, though it really only had been a few days. I turned the handle and passed the threshold. Stevenson was deeply asleep in the middle of the floor on his back with a book over his face, breathing incredibly loudly.

I walked as quietly past him as I could; it wouldn't have mattered if I was making noise - he could sleep through almost anything these days. I went to my bed a room over and laid down, looking up at the light. Those damned lights still bothered me, so I rolled to face the wall and pulled the blanket over my head. *There, sleep, have your way.*

"I've got it!" I yelled loudly, sitting up so fast that the room spun. "I have *finally* figured it out..." This was a whisper, just to myself.

Rushing out the door, I nearly tripped myself into a concussion, but I caught myself just in time and only ended up with some cut up hands. It didn't bother me though, nothing could bother me right now. I dusted my hands and kept hurtling to the back wall, and about half way there my stomach lurched and yelled at me to turn around and get some sustenance. *Shut up!* I thought down to it.

I paused there for a moment. *Great...* I thought sarcastically. *Now all I can think about is food.* I rolled my eyes and started off in the other direction.

Some of the people in the cafeteria looked at me funny as I scarfed down my food so fast that I actually choked on it. I waved my hand at them dismissively before leaving like my butt was lit up with flames.

I was out of breath by the time I got down the second flight of stairs, pausing to catch my breath before jogging to the desk to start shuffling through the drawer of De's old notes.

"Where is it... I know I've seen it somewhere around here." I kept digging, and it took me what felt like forever to find the specific folder of De's notes. Up until last night, I had thought of it as nothing more than the insane ramblings of a elderly man.

But under this new light... It was the answer I had been looking for, the one that even the doctor himself had dismissed. But this was it. It was what both of us had spent so long now searching for. This stack of crazed scribbles held together by too many paperclips was the answer to finding the cure.

I worked away, getting lost again in the motions of it all, although this time it was with a new strength. I must have been down there for days, because Stevenson had to come for me to make sure I wasn't dead. He set some food down as I was trying to lift papers up. I looked at him, and his eyes widened. I must have been a horrible sight to see.

"When's the last time you ate? Or slept?" he asked quite frustratedly. "Or showered?"

"This morning...?" My voice must have gone up a minimum of an octave when I said this, very unsure of the truth of it. He looked at me, disbelieving. I sighed. "The last morning that I was outside..." My voice trailed off.

"How long ago was that?" His deep voice grew louder. He was clearly done with my crap.

"...I'm not... *entirely* sure." I mumbled and turned in the chair to face away from him and to stand. He sighed loudly and so gutturally, it almost sounded like a growl. I stood up and turned to him, holding the chair to keep me steady and keep the dizziness from dropping me to the floor. "I'm close -"

"Bullshit," he cut me off. "De was 'close' and look where that got him. Just give up, just stop. Accept that there isn't a cure before you rot away." He waved his hand in my direction, gesturing at my current disheveled state.

I just looked at him, staring him down until my eyes burned. He exhaled, and his entire face softened, the anger leaving him because he knew why I couldn't 'just stop'. He walked around the chair and hugged me.

"Eat, please," Stevenson pleaded with me quickly before leaving.

I did as he asked. I ate and slept, knowing full well that I couldn't think enough to find a cure if I was this tired. When I woke up and had a full stomach, it was much easier to read De's handwriting. I pulled out a few more vials and tried several different combinations with the written instructions.

"I did it..."

Stevenson woke up, not to my words, but because I was shaking him like the world was ending. It wasn't ending - it already had - no, now the world was *beginning*.

"Did what?" he asked in a half-asleep daze.

"I figured it out. I found the cure." He sat up, definitely awake now.

"Are you certain?"

"Almost a hundred percent. But I need your help to test it." He nodded while standing up and stumbling to put on shoes. "I want to make a quick stop first though, to pay an old bastard a visit." He slowed the process of tying his shoes and looked at me strangely.

We went outside of The Camp's walls to a large patch of graves. I knew exactly where De was buried, and beelined it to the small rock I had placed as a headstone. I squatted down. Stevenson stayed far enough back to not hear me.

"Thank you," I said genuinely, setting my hand down on the stone before standing and nodding to the young man for us to walk back.

I grabbed a vial off of the desk, one I had been working with and had the most faith in. Taking a syringe, I filled it with some of what I genuinely believed to be the cure and pulled the keys out to unlock Beck's cage. Stevenson grabbed the chair and some zip ties, then followed me in.

Beck had just woken up, but he wrestled against Stevenson, cussing and lashing out as best as his restraints would let him. Stevenson stood back, wiping his hands down his face. He dropped them, and in this light, the scar on his right hand was hard to miss.

Beck was finally strapped down to the chair. He had pulled out his IV, which was how he had been getting nutrients and would be testing the cure. We put it back in.

"It's not gonna work. It'll never work. I'll die, and you'll have to watch every damn moment of it." He smiled and started laughing. He was once Beck. Some of Beck was still in there, and he knew how to cut me deep.

I did my best to keep from reacting and letting him know he was successful in his attempts to hurt me. I emptied the syringe into his IV and waited. Nothing happened at first, but after a moment Beck's head seemed to be too heavy and started swaying from side to side before it fell forward.

I swallowed hard, trying my best to not think of all of the ways that this could go wrong. *Just fucking calm down, Jelli.*

When he lifted his head to us again, the mark on his cheek was gone and his beautiful brown eyes looked up and me then darted around the room, confused. He started panicking. "Where - where is she?" he asked, pulling against his ties.

"Where is who?" I said through the shock of the sight of Beck's real eyes.

"Where *is* she?!" He was angry, his voice scared and demanding. He pulled against his restraints hard enough to almost knock the chair over. Stevenson grabbed the chair and forced it still, Beck looked at him and made a face lacking any recognition. He turned his head to me and begged again. "Where is she?"

"Beck, where is who?"

He spoke like it was obvious what he was asking, like I should simply *know* to whom he was referring. I wasn't the one without knowledge though. Beck had forgotten it all...

"Where is Sammy?"

Enjoy the book?

Keep an eye out for *Raspberries*, the next book in the saga.

Coming April 2025.

Turn the page to read the first chapter.

Chapter One

I leaned over the edge of her side of the bed, kissing her lightly on the forehead. She rustled a little at the touch and groaned what was meant to be words. It always brought a smile to my face the way that she tried to speak when she was so deeply asleep. "Good morning, Love." I all but breathed the words as I stood back up and walked to the door of our room. She mumbled something again and rolled over, my smile deepened and I closed the door leaving her again in the darkness, to let her rest.

I left my fingers around the handle for a moment and let out a sigh, every bone in my body begged me to go back to bed and lay with my wife until well after the sun would rise. But I was needed at work.

My car struggled to start at first. Please, not today. I prayed wordlessly through closed, tired eyes. It rumbled to life and the little spark of worry flitted from my chest.

There was no traffic, as always, with working such an early shift came empty roads and slow, dark drives. It was a nice, peaceful way to start the day, but in many ways almost too peaceful. The empty roads and twinkling lights in the distance would almost lull me to sleep every day, I would turn up the radio and sip on water to keep myself awake. I knew it was bad to drive drowsy, but alone on the roads and with so little sleep I didn't have much of a choice.

I pulled into the parking lot. My hands slid down from the steering wheel and onto my lap while my eyes pulled up to the buzzing neon lights of the fast food dump that I worked at.

It was a real low point in my working career, but the cushy job I had with the city had laid me off a few months before and this was the first place that I could get to hire me. Although having a job wasn't the biggest worry in the world, with my wife having such a good teaching position as she did at the local college. But having a second income did make us worry less about bills and made taking care of our little family a bit easier.

I straightened my shoulders in a stretch and left the warmth of my car to walk through the crisp, cool air of the early morning.

I worked the earliest shift of a little twenty four hour food joint, called 'Patty's patties'. It was always slow on my shift, but it gave me a chance to clean and stock the place for the people who would work the rushes. Like always, my day dragged on and on, ever so slowly. By the time I got off just after noon, I smelt of burgers, grease and fries, I always hated that about working there.
There was traffic on my way home, it never bothered me too much but today it did get to me a little. I so badly just wanted to be back at my house and in a hot shower with my wife.

The whiteboard on the wall by the calendar said that she had stepped out to go grocery shopping and would be back soon. Alone I guess. I checked my watch but didn't read the time and made my way to the master bedroom. I stripped down and out of the cheap uniform that I was required to wear and stood under the water until it began to run cold.

I ran my forearm against the mirror to clear away the fog. I stared at my reflection, rubbing my hand against the stubble that had been creeping up on my face for the past few days. I preferred to be clean shaven, but my wife would always call my beard sexy so I only glanced at the razor by the sink before deciding that it was worth the itchiness.

My wife came in with two armfuls of groceries, laying them on the kitchen table. I leaned in to kiss her, she gave me a peck on the cheek instead and spoke before turning again to leave. "Gotta get the boys from school, I'll be back soon. Put those away for me will you?"

"Will do." I smiled after her. "I love you, Honey, drive safely please."

"I love you too." She shouted, before closing the door behind her.

Alone again.

I put the food away and made some peanut butter and jelly sandwiches for the boys to have as an after school snack while they do their homework.

This is how most every weekday went. I'd go to work before anyone woke up, I would see my wife in passing and we would pass off who would go to get our sons from school. They would do homework when they got home before their mother went to work and we ate dinner as a family. On the weekends we would watch movies together or go out on little family field trips sometimes. It was a simple routine but it worked for us.

Little did I know, that would be the last day like that. Our little world would come crumbling down, the last Tuesday of the life I had grown so fond to know.

I should have cherished it.

"Dad! James is breathing really loud right next to me! Make him stop it!" Junior whined to me, running into the living room.

"He's what now?" I set down the book that was in my hands and glanced past my son to the kitchen to check the timer for the lasagna.

"He is breathing too loud!" He shouted again.

"I don't know what he's talking about... I'm just minding my own business." My elder son said, walking in after his younger brother.

"He's lying!"

"Am not." James leaned in close to his younger brother and exhaled heavily by his ear. "I'm just breathing."

"See, Dad, he did it again!" Junior screamed now, pointing and flailing his arms at his brother.

I sighed. Setting my book on the table next to me. "Leave your brother alone. Go do your homework or something." I said, setting my hand on James' head and guiding him away from Junior.

"Already done."

"Then go play outside until dinner is done. Don't go too far, I'll call you when it's ready."

"Cool." He jumped up and ran toward the back of the house, came out with his skateboard in hand and headed for the front door.

"As for you, go play in your room." Junior scoffed, grumbling something under his breath about how unfair it was that James got to go outside and he had to go to his room. Reluctantly, however, he listened and went as instructed.

I sunk back down into the couch, not picking up my book again, it was boring me anyhow.

My boys were always like this, picking fights with each other about anything under the sun, but even still the both of them were my whole world.

The timer for the oven went off, shocking me out of my empty thoughts. I shook my head, now manually breathing, and stood to turn it off and pull dinner out to start to cool. I reached for the button and as my fingers grazed it the front door swung open and my son screamed for me. "Dad! Dad, you need to see this!" I pressed the button to stop the beeping and hear him better. I turned to see the genuine fear in his eyes.

"What's going on?" I stepped forward toward him. "What's wrong?"

He struggled to catch his breath. "Outside... I- it's- something just happened..." I jogged to the window to see what his sentences couldn't describe.

I pulled back the curtain just in time to see my gentle, elderly neighbor slit his wife's throat across the street. He turned around looking at his surroundings as she fell to the ground clutching her neck. I leaned back so that he couldn't see me, but as his face came into full view beneath the streetlight I saw paint mixed with a little bit of blood on his face. "God have mercy... What is happening?" I thought in an audible whisper.

My older son walked to my side, I pulled him behind me. "Stay away from the window." I warned him sternly. Jankens would never hurt his wife... he would never hurt anyone... I grabbed the back of James' shirt and walked him through the kitchen, down the hall and to his brother's room. "Don't move, not until I come for you, and don't open this door for anyone but me." I didn't know what was happening, but I knew I had to protect my sons.

I walked again to the window at the front of the house, Jankens had disappeared from my view, it was freshly dark outside, the sun had just set, so the houses were starting to fall into shadow. I couldn't place why, but this only worried me more. I snuck back into the room with the boys, sat down with them against the far wall and pulled them into a hug.

"Dad, what's going on? I'm scared." Junior whimpered beneath my arm.

"I don't know..." I whispered. "But don't worry, we'll be okay." I squeezed them tighter to me and leaned down to kiss them both on top of their heads. I didn't know if what I was saying was the truth, but I needed it to be. I bowed my head and began to pray. Please, protect my sons, keep them safe, let them be unscathed by- my prayer was cut short by a loud scream outside of the window and a bright, sudden, orange glow of flames.

My younger son began to cry loudly, I rubbed his back and shushed him, though it did little good. My older son got very still, his face went white and his lower lip quivered, slowly, ever so slowly, his eyes drifted up to meet mine. I couldn't bear to see the look they held, so I shut mine tight and pressed my forehead against his. "It'll be alright." I promised emptily.

A moment passed, only not silent because of the noises of violence which drifted in from throughout the neighborhood. James asked a question, a question I hadn't let myself think before he voiced it. "What about Mom?"

I sucked in a breath and swallowed hard, forcing the images that flooded my mind out. "She'll be okay." She has to be.

We sat like that for a long time, my son's night light illuminating the concern on our faces in a ghostly manner. I rolled my wrist to check the time of my watch. She should be back by now... All three of our heads shot up at the sound of breaking glass outside, my sons burying their faces against me again when the next sound, a rustling inside the house, was heard.

    I pulled myself out of their desperate embraces. Unplugged the unused lamp on my son's night table and wrapped the cord around my arm before tightly gripping its base in my hand. I turned back to my boys, placing a finger over my mouth before holding an open hand out to them. Motioning for them to stay put and stay quiet. I grabbed the door knob and snuck out into the hall.

    My wife pulled me into a hug right outside the door. "Honey..." She spoke into me. "Out there... Everyone has gone... mad..." I let the lamp all but fall out of my grip and pulled her tighter against me. "The boys?!" She pushed away and stared at me, tears running down her face.

    I nodded. "They're safe." I opened the door and pulled her into the room, uniting the family once again. She ran to her sons, fell to the ground, and hugged them with a kind of love only a mother could. I closed the door behind me and slid to the floor. I unwound the lamp's cord from my arm and dropped it, leaning back against the wood and running my hands through my hair.

    Please, God, what is going on?

    We sat like that for a long time, listening to the world fall into chaos outside of our four walls of safety. I heard a rustling to my left and opened my eyes to see my beautiful, worried Alyssa crawling across the carpet to my side. She rested her hand on my arm and her eyes clung to me in a way that made me feel sure and safe again. I raised my right hand to her face, noting the marks that the wire had made as I wiped tear marks from her cheeks.

    The fire alarm began to ring, ruining the comfort that we had all begun to settle into. I jumped up, held my hand out to my wife when she too went to stand. I fled from the room and to the kitchen. I pulled the burning lasagna out from the oven and threw it onto the stove before shutting it off. I grabbed the nearest chair to get closer to the fire alarm in the kitchen, waving one of the oven mitts in its direction to clear away some of the smoke.

Acknowledgements

Thank you Breyanna and Imogen, for teaching me to love reading and for supporting me through my writing.

www.ingramcontent.com/pod-product-compliance
Lightning Source LLC
LaVergne TN
LVHW031605060526
838201LV00063B/4736